"I'd like to see you in the silver lace," Philip drawled, loosening his tie and unbuttoning the top of his shirt.

It was a dream of a dress. She went behind the screen and slipped it on quickly. Looking down at herself, she realized that it was shockingly bare. Nervously, she stepped out and stood in front of Philip. "Here it is. Not right for tomorrow night, I think—and I'd definitely need a slip."

Philip's breath caught in his throat. The lines of her body were clearly visible beneath the silver lace, and she looked as if she were wearing a shimmering cobweb. "I like it," he managed to say, walking over to her. "How does it fit?" he asked, reaching out and skimming a finger beneath one fragile strap to caress the smooth skin of her shoulder.

She froze, unable even to draw a breath. "Fine."

He hooked his finger around the strap and tugged at it. "Not too tight?" She shook her head. "Because I wouldn't want it to dig into your skin."

"It doesn't." She could barely speak, her throat was so tight.

He pulled the strap off her shoulder and released it, then smoothed a finger back and forth over her bare shoulder where the strap had been. Then, with brooding intensity, he brushed the edge of the neckline, his fingers caressing her pale flesh. "This is low, isn't it?"

"Yes," she whispered.

"The material looks like it's made of moon rays." He continued to delve deeper inside the neckline, making heat throb through her body. "You should have only the softest materials against your skin—silk, satin, velvet. . . ."

She closed her eyes as his hands ignited a desire that engulfed her in flames. . . .

WHAT ARE *LOVESWEPT* ROMANCES?

They are stories of true romance and touching emotion. We believe those two very important ingredients are constants in our highly sensual and very believable stories in the *LOVESWEPT* line. Our goal is to give you, the reader, stories of consistently high quality that may sometimes make you laugh, sometimes make you cry, but are always fresh and creative and contain many delightful surprises within their pages.

Most romance fans read an enormous number of books. Those they truly love, they keep. Others may be traded with friends and soon forgotten. We hope that each *LOVESWEPT* romance will be a treasure—a "keeper." We will always try to publish

LOVE STORIES YOU'LL NEVER FORGET
BY AUTHORS YOU'LL ALWAYS REMEMBER

The Editors

Loveswept® 573

Fayrene Preston
In the Heat of the Night

BANTAM BOOKS
NEW YORK · TORONTO · LONDON · SYDNEY · AUCKLAND

IN THE HEAT OF THE NIGHT
A Bantam Book / October 1992

*If you would be interested in receiving protective vinyl
covers for your Loveswept books, please write to this address
for information:*

*Loveswept
Bantam Books
P.O. Box 985
Hicksville, NY 11802*

ISBN 0-553-44172-8

Published simultaneously in the United States and Canada

Bantam Books are published by Bantam Books, a division of
Bantam Doubleday Dell Publishing Group, Inc. Its trademark,
consisting of the words "Bantam Books" and the portrayal of
a rooster, is Registered in U.S. Patent and Trademark Office
and in other countries. Marca Registrada. Bantam Books, 666
Fifth Avenue, New York, New York 10103.

In the Heat of the Night

Prologue

In the large book-lined study, a single lamp glowed. It spread light over the gleaming mahogany desk and illuminated the fax Philip Killane had received minutes before. He stared hard at the words, trying to understand why they unsettled him so.

I'm coming home. Jacey.

He heard the grandfather clock in the entry hall strike twelve; he reached for his coffee and sipped the hot brew.

Over the years, Jacey had sent other telegrams and faxes to the house. She always stated her arrival and departure dates and indicated whether she would be staying at her apartment in the city or if she would be coming out to the house. But this fax had none of that information.

He should go to bed, he thought, tossing the fax onto his desk. But he continued to stare at the piece of paper.

I'm coming home. It was an odd phrase for her to use.

He barely knew her, but he found it hard to

believe that she viewed this house as home, the Georgian mansion on the Hudson where she had come to live when she was thirteen years old, the time of the marriage of his father to her mother.

When she did come here, she usually stayed no more than a day, two at the most, visiting with her mother and going out of her way to avoid him whenever possible.

Toying with the coffee cup, he looked at the fax again. She had sent it from Bombay, India. Another faraway place. Jacey specialized in faraway places.

I'm coming home.

Could it be remotely possible that she really meant it? And if so, what were her motives?

Wearily he leaned his head back against the leather chair and closed his eyes. A picture of Jacey swam into his mind, Jacey with her icy aqua eyes and cool beauty. She hated him. But the knowledge didn't stop his blood from stirring, because in the recesses of his mind he carried another image of her, an image seared into his brain from a long time ago, when she had been warm, soft, and sweet, and so hot, he had nearly incinerated.

His eyes flew open and he hit the desk with a closed fist. Dammit, the message had been carelessly worded, that's all. She didn't mean it. He prayed she didn't. Because if she did, it was the worst possible time for her to be coming home.

One

Five Days Later

"Mrs. Killane wants to know if you'll be down for breakfast."

Philip Killane glanced at Barton, the man who had been the Killane family butler for as long as he could remember. Barton was so discreet and reserved, he sometimes seemed almost nonexistent. But two generations of Killanes had depended on him, first his father and now him.

With a grin Philip straightened his tie. Both he and Barton knew that he very rarely ate breakfast with Edith, but each morning she sent Barton to his room to inquire of his plans. Propriety was of the utmost importance to his stepmother, and she always waited for him. "I can't this morning. Tell her I'll get something at the office."

"Yes, sir."

He reached for his suit jacket, but paused when he heard a car come up the driveway. "Hold on a minute, Barton." He walked to the window, pulled aside the curtain, and looked down. Below in the courtyard, a limousine eased to a stop, and the uniformed driver got out and hurried around the car to open the passenger door.

Long, shapely legs appeared from the depths of the limousine. Silvery-blue high heels touched the bricked driveway. A gold and pearl bracelet glinted and crimson nails gleamed as a hand reached out and grasped the driver's arm, then a slender blonde slid out, wearing a Chanel suit the exact color of the high heels.

Philip turned away from the window, his face and voice without expression. "Inform Mrs. Killane that her daughter has arrived."

Jacey looked up at the house and saw the curtain fall back into place. Philip. She felt herself sway and placed her hand on top of the car to steady herself. She had known she was going to have to see him, but now that she was here, she wondered if she should have waited a few more weeks. Even as the thought occurred, she banished it. She had very definite reasons for coming home now, and she intended to see this visit through.

The front door opened, and Barton, a welcoming smile on his distinguished face, walked out to help the driver with her bags.

With effort she squared her shoulders and entered the house.

Crossing the polished marble floor of the entry hall to its center, she reflected that no matter how long she stayed away from this place, she could always count on it to remain just as she remembered it. In an ever-changing world, nothing was ever changed or moved in this house. She was reassured by the fact, though there were many who would be surprised to know she felt that way.

The faint scent of lemon oil hung in the air.

Fresh flowers in a Steuben vase graced a table beneath a gold-framed mirror. A portrait of Marcus Killane hung on one wall. When she was home, she often saw her mother standing before the portrait of her late husband, staring up at it. In Jacey's more fanciful moments she had sometimes thought that Marcus was talking to her mother, though Marcus had been dead for five years. But if there was a way to communicate after death, she knew Marcus would find it.

The driver set the last of her bags down and handed her a clipboard with an attached receipt. After looking it over, she signed it, frowning as she noticed that her hands were shaking.

Behind her she heard the sound of steady, self-assured footsteps descending the staircase.

She returned the clipboard with a quiet thank-you, and then, with spine straight, she turned to face Philip. In the few seconds she had before he reached her, her senses came alive in a way they did only for him, and she registered a myriad of things about him. He was tall and lean, with an elegance that seemed to have been born in him, though she still could remember a time when he had fairly exploded with energy, impatience, and impulsiveness. Now, as befitted a man accustomed to authority and command, his movements were controlled and thoughtful, and his broad shoulders carried a mantle of power as easily as they did his Armani suit. But one thing had never changed. Every bone, cell, and square inch of tissue of his body was imbued with a sensuality that always appeared to her as being a breath away from bursting free from his golden-beige skin.

He stopped in front of her, and his dark brown eyes lasered through her. "Hello, Jacey. I'd say you were looking well, but you're not. Your skin is so pale, I can almost see through it, and there are purple smudges under your eyes."

She clasped her now badly shaking hands together. "Hello, Philip. Charming as ever, I see." In fact, he could be charming, with anyone other than herself.

"I don't give compliments. I state facts." He paused. "Jet lag?"

"Yes," she said without hesitation. "Jet lag."

He nodded. "With as many time zones as you cross in any given year, I'm surprised you don't look worse."

Her smile didn't reach her eyes. "Be careful. That was almost a compliment, backhanded though it might be."

He laughed softly and with faint menace. "It, too, was only a statement of fact." He glanced at the pile of suitcases Barton had set by the door. "It looks as if you're moving in."

"I'll be staying for a while."

"Really? How unusual."

"Don't get nervous. It won't be permanent."

His eyes narrowed. "I honestly didn't think it would be. You have an aversion for staying in any one place too long. Especially here. Your frequent-flyer miles must be in the high seven figures by now."

"Eight, actually. Is Mother here?"

"She's in the breakfast room. She's looking forward to seeing you."

Her lips twisted into a weary grin, and she threw a pointed glance around the entry hall where only the two of them stood. "Yes, I can tell."

"You know your mother."

She sighed. "Yes, I do. Very well. I'll go in to see her." She hesitated. She had things to say to him, but she had given the matter some thought and had decided it would be best to wait until she was more rested. "Do you plan to be home for dinner tonight?"

His expression mocked her. "Do you have some reason for asking?"

She didn't care if her legs felt as if they were about to fold beneath her; she refused to show any weakness. "Do you have some reason for not answering?"

He smiled. "Prickly as ever, aren't you? I had every intention of answering you, Jacey. I was just curious, that's all. The reasons you do things have never been very clear to me, but then, you've seen to it that we've never been around each other very much."

For a split second she felt rooted to the floor, rooted there by his mocking arrogance, his cutting sarcasm, his sheer physical presence. Then she moved, heading for the door that would lead her to the breakfast room.

As she passed him, his hand snaked out, closed around her upper arm, and stopped her in her tracks. Her head spun at the abrupt cessation of her movement, and she swayed against him. Automatically his body supported her weight, his free hand sliding around her waist to her back to steady her.

Pressed against his hard body from her breasts to thighs, she could feel the movement of his muscles as they tensed and rippled. Hot and cold shivers ran through her. She quivered, fighting against the madness of wanting to stay exactly where she was.

"Jacey?"

His voice had turned soft and husky, giving the impression of a vaporous cloud of sensuality descending over her. She placed her hands against his chest, intending to push away from him, but she felt the pounding of his heart beneath her palms. The strong, steady rhythm transfixed her.

"Jacey?"

His voice sounded even softer. She almost weakened then, almost lost what little composure remained. But drawing on equal measures of fear and pride, she pulled herself together and straightened away from him. To her dismay, her breasts tingled where they had touched him; she crossed her arms beneath them.

He stared at her with a frown on his face. "Are you all right?"

"Of course. I just lost my balance."

"Okay," he said, accepting her explanation but continuing to study her as if she were a book.

His concentration on her endangered her already overburdened nervous system. "What do you want?"

A strange expression flickered in his eyes. "Want?"

She tried to swallow but couldn't. Nerves had constricted her throat. As usual, her instincts were telling her to get away from him. "Why did you stop me?" she finally managed to ask.

He released his hold on her arm. "I wanted to answer your question. I plan to be home for dinner tonight unless something unexpected comes up . . . or unless you would prefer I find something else to do."

Her lips tightened. "Don't be silly. This is your home."

"It's your home too."

She hadn't lived there in many years, but strangely enough she did consider this house her home. "I'll see you tonight, Philip."

"I'll look forward to it, Jacey."

As if on cue, Barton reappeared and handed Philip's briefcase to him. With a nod of thanks to the man and one last look at Jacey, Philip left.

Jacey stared at the door after it shut behind him, disturbed to discover that in her mind Philip's image was still as vivid as if he were standing in front of her. In fact, she could still feel his magnetic energy, just the way she had always been able to feel it, no matter how hard she fought against it, no matter how far away from him she went. Only a discreet cough from Barton brought her back to her surroundings.

"I'll have your luggage taken up to your room immediately. In the meantime your mother is waiting for you in the breakfast room. Shall I lead the way?"

She smiled faintly. "Believe it or not, Barton, I do still remember where it is, but thank you."

"You're welcome, miss, and may I say it's good to have you home again."

Her smile widened, because she knew Barton's sentiments were sincere. And because he was the only one who she was sure felt that way.

As she entered the breakfast room, her mother raised her head, switching her attention from the morning paper to her daughter. An annoyed lift of her brow told Jacey she had been expected sooner. Her mother's words confirmed it.

"Jacey darling, at last."

Jacey fixed a smile on her face and walked the length of the table to bestow a kiss on her mother's porcelain-perfect cheek. It didn't matter that her mother hadn't finished breakfast yet. She was already dressed in the silk dress in which she would no doubt attend the day's scheduled luncheon, and her hair was coiffed into its classic chin-length well-sprayed pageboy, a style she had worn for as long as Jacey could remember.

"It's good to see you, Mother." It was true. Though it had been years since she and her mother had been able to get along, Jacey loved her. One of the things she hoped to accomplish by coming home was to make some kind of peace with her. She wanted to get to the point where her mother's constant picking didn't bother her so much. In fact, she wished that the two of them could learn to enjoy each other, maybe even become friends. It was an extremely large wish.

"It's good to see you too, darling, though, I must say, you aren't looking your best."

It was beginning. Jacey sighed and sank down into a chair at an angle to the one her mother sat in. "Too many airplanes. You know how dry the air is on a plane."

"Yes, I do. That's why I haven't made an avocation out of traveling, and I don't understand why you have. Anyone with half an eye can see the devastating effect it's had on your skin."

"I enjoy traveling," she said, her tone deliberately mild.

"Yes, and I can see the result. Darling, you really do look *dreadful*."

Jacey couldn't help but smile. Nothing ever changed. Gaining peace was definitely going to be an uphill battle. But then, she had known that. "Yes, so Philip just informed me."

"Oh, I'm glad you got to see him before he left for work. He stays so busy, it's almost an occasion when I get to see him myself, and we live in the same house."

"I'm sure you're exaggerating. Philip said he would be home this evening for dinner."

Edith picked up her coffee cup and daintily sipped at it. "Then it's in your honor, not mine."

"I seriously doubt that," Jacey said, determinedly ignoring the faint resentment in her mother's voice and hurrying on before she could retort. "Tell me what you've been up to these days. You look beautiful this morning. Are you going anywhere special today?"

"Yes, I'm having lunch at the club with the girls. We're planning a little charity event for the hospital."

Thankful that her diversionary tactics worked, Jacey gave a quick smile to the maid who poured her a cup of coffee. "That should be fun. You and your friends always do an excellent job of raising money for good causes."

"Yes, we do." Edith's eyes narrowed, a sign that Jacey's diversion had worked only temporarily. "Your fax wasn't as precise as usual. It gave no departure date."

She stared down at the steaming liquid in her cup. It had been a mistake to get up so early and drive from the city. Her intention had been to get the relatively short trip over with, but she had overestimated her stamina. Philip and her mother might think she looked bad, but getting herself to look as good as she did had been a major effort. And at the moment she didn't feel strong enough to lift the cup to her lips. Besides, the caffeine wouldn't help her. "That's because I have no definite plans right now."

"You mean you don't know how long you're going to stay?"

"No. . . ." She looked at her mother. "I'd like to stay here awhile, that is, if you don't mind."

"Mind? Why should I mind? I'd *love* it if you

would stay. If you'll remember, I never wanted you to leave in the first place."

"Yes, Mother, I know. I remember."

"And do you also remember—"

Jacey summoned her remaining strength and stood. "Since you have plans for the day, I think I'll go up to my room and lie down for a few hours."

Her mother frowned. "Lie down? At this time of day?"

She used her standard excuse. "Jet lag. It can be so draining."

"I'm sure *no* one knows that as well as you." The brackets on either side of Edith's mouth deepened with disapproval, but her voice held reluctant sympathy. "The flight must have taken forever."

Unwilling at the moment to admit that she had returned from Bombay the day before yesterday and had rested at her New York City apartment for a full day, she simply said, "Yes, it did."

"Well, maybe a little nap wouldn't hurt, then."

Jacey eyed the distance between her and her mother and decided kissing her again wasn't worth the effort. Instead, she carefully walked toward the door. "Have a good day, Mother. I'll see you this evening."

Jacey awoke slowly. At first the now-familiar lethargy that had been a part of her for the past two and a half months kept her from opening her eyes. She listened for the commonplace sounds she had grown accustomed to, sounds of nurses and visitors passing in the hallway, medicine and food carts being pushed from one room to the other, doctors conferring. But all she heard was quiet.

Slowly she opened her eyes, and the bedroom

that had been hers from the time she was thirteen until she had gone away to college swam into view. The teddy bear that her daddy had given her when she was four years old still sat on the window seat. A picture of her in her senior year cheerleading outfit hung on the wall beside her dresser mirror. Another picture on the opposite side of the mirror was of her and the group of friends she had hung out with in high school.

She was no longer in that white, sterile room in the hospital in Bombay, she realized.

With a silent, fervent prayer of thanks, she rolled her head on the pillow so that she could gaze out the window. It was dusk. She wasn't surprised she had slept the day away. Since she had come down with the strange virus that had almost taken her life, she slept most of the time. The long hours of sleep had allowed her body to begin repairing itself. She was much better now, but the trip from Bombay to New York and then here to the house on the Hudson had taken a lot out of her.

When she had been lying in that hospital bed in Bombay, too weak to do anything else but listen to the doctors argue over what could be wrong with her and whether she was going to live or die, she had come to the decision that if she ever regained her strength, she would come home and try to straighten out her life.

It had seemed like such a good idea. In fact, at times it was all that had kept her drawing her next breath. But she had been away so long that she had forgotten certain things, *important* things, such as how her mother's acerbic tongue seemed to worsen whenever she was in the same room with her. And the devastating effect Philip could have on her nervous system. Had always had.

• • •

Midway through the impeccably cooked and served dinner, Edith sipped from her wineglass and smiled approvingly at Philip, who sat opposite her at the head of the table. "Excellent choice, Philip."

"Thank you. I thought a special wine was called for this evening since we have a special guest."

Jacey pushed her food around on her plate and tried to ignore the jab he had directed at her. This morning he had said this was her home. Tonight he was calling her a guest. She wasn't surprised, though. Philip's feelings for her had never been consistent.

His lids were hooded as he looked at her. "You haven't tried the wine yet, Jacey."

"I just haven't gotten around to it. I will." Actually drinking of any kind wouldn't have been good for her at this stage of her recovery, but she hadn't been able to come up with a reason to refuse the wine that wouldn't have prompted more questions.

She felt her mother's eagle-eyed gaze on her and braced for another volley.

"First thing in the morning I'm going to book you in for a day at Elizabeth Arden."

Her lips twitched. "Do you really think a day will be enough, Mother?"

"Yes, of course—" Edith stopped, realizing Jacey was making light of her idea. "It's obvious you've been neglecting your skin, darling. A day might not be enough, but it will certainly be a good beginning."

Jacey stole a quick glance at Philip from beneath her lashes and saw that he was frowning at the contents of his wineglass. The ends of his hair were wet and his face carried a five o'clock shadow, as if he'd taken a hurried shower before dinner but hadn't had time to shave. She found the sign of masculinity unnerving. "Thank you for your concern, Mother, but I think I'll hold off on Elizabeth Arden for a while."

"Suit yourself. I was only trying to be helpful."

"I appreciate it." She studied the food on her plate and decided to try the mashed potatoes—something soft and easily digestible. Even though her appetite had gradually improved over the past few weeks, she was finding it hard to eat with her mother on one side of her and Philip on the other. They were her only remaining family, but unfortunately they were also her adversaries.

"Darling," her mother said in a tone that managed to be both pointed and pained, "it's been so long since you've had dinner with us, you must have forgotten. Philip and I always dress for dinner."

She was amazed her mother had waited as long as she had to remark on the loose-fitting silk caftan she had chosen to wear. And she hadn't forgotten her mother's idea of what was and wasn't proper attire to wear to the dinner table. She just hadn't felt equal to putting on anything that would require stockings and high heels. Besides, she really didn't have too many things that wouldn't emphasize the weight she had lost in the last couple of months.

"Sorry, Mother. I haven't unpacked yet, and I didn't think you'd mind just this once."

"No, of course not, it's just that—"

"Jacey looks lovely as always, Edith," Philip remarked casually. "It doesn't matter what she wears. Never has."

Both Jacey and her mother looked at him in surprise.

Suddenly Jacey remembered when she had first come to this house to live. She had felt gawky, awkward, and ugly. He had been seventeen, and occasionally, in the careless, offhand way of a teenage boy, he would throw out a remark to defend her from her mother's critical barbs. She had thought he was wonderful. She smiled at him. "Thank you, Philip."

His dark eyes were enigmatic. "I was simply stating a fact. I'm sure you hear it a lot."

"Jacey is a beautiful young woman," Edith said, agreeing with him, then turned to her daughter. "But you seem way too thin. I hope you're not dieting. I know a great many people feel one cannot be too thin, but if you lose any more weight, you'll look like a scarecrow."

Her smile slipped only slightly. "Do you think if you tried really hard, Mother, you might be able, just *once*, to give me a compliment without tacking on a but."

Edith's eyes widened. "Why, I don't know what you're talking about. I want only the best for you. It's all I've ever wanted."

Philip stirred in his chair, drawing her gaze. "Is there some significance to the timing of your visit, Jacey?"

"No, not really."

She didn't want either her mother or him to know how seriously ill she had been. She wasn't up to hearing yet another lecture from her mother on the dangers of traveling to third world countries where the amenities weren't up to the standards of the United States. And she didn't want to see disdain in Philip's eyes at her stupidity for drinking bad water, or putting herself in the way of a virus-carrying insect, or whatever it was she had done to become infected. And though she didn't think either of them would be so inclined, above all, she didn't want to risk being on the receiving end of their sympathy. Her goal was to be able to exist peacefully with them without bitterness, without hurt. And if she was to be successful, she had to meet them as equals.

"You didn't run out of countries to visit or anything like that?" Philip asked.

"No, nothing like that." She paused, then said pleasantly, "Tell me, what do you two do for conversation when I'm not here to grill?"

"We're not grilling you, darling. We're just interested, that's all. Aren't we, Philip?"

He lifted his wineglass to his lips. "Absolutely fascinated."

Jacey didn't miss the sarcasm in Philip's voice, but apparently Edith did, because she went on. "The last time we saw you was . . . was it last Christmas?"

Most mothers would remember whether their only child had spent Christmas with them, Jacey thought wryly. Not hers, though.

She shook her head. "No. I spent Christmas in Switzerland with friends, but I did fly in for your birthday last year."

Edith nodded. "Oh, that's right. I met you in the city, and we had dinner together."

With an idle movement of his wrist, Philip twirled the wine in his glass. "But I didn't see you then. In fact, I can't remember the last time I did see you."

She could. It had been three years before. His hair had been longer. He hadn't looked as tired. They had barely spoken. "I barged in on your company picnic. Remember? There were hundreds of people on the lawn." Including a leggy redhead who had seemed to find it hard to let him out of her sight.

"How could you barge in, Jacey? This is your home."

One minute he was being kind, the next he was slicing her in two with his sarcasm. Her nerves rebelled. "Make up your mind, Philip. A few minutes ago you were calling me a guest."

"Forgive me but since I see you only once every few years or so, I tend to get confused about just what you are."

Edith cleared her throat, a nervous habit whenever any sort of tension threatened to disrupt her perfect surroundings. "Since you're going to be staying awhile, Jacey, I think it would be a splendid idea if we gave a party. There are so many people who would love to see you, and—"

"I don't think so, Mother. I'm not in a party mood."

Philip's eyebrows arched. "Now, there's something new."

Old resentments flared, catching her unaware. "I don't think you're in any position to say what is or isn't new for me."

"You're absolutely right," he said smoothly, tonelessly. "I stand corrected."

She bit her bottom lip. Dammit, bickering with him was the last thing she wanted. "I'm sorry. I guess I'm still a little tired."

"There's no need to apologize. You were only pointing out the obvious."

"Still—"

"Forget it." His eyes glinted with an expression she couldn't read. "Instead, why don't you tell me why you're tired? Barton said you slept all day."

Edith nodded. "That's true. You were still asleep when I got back from the club."

"You both checked on me?" she asked, incredulous. She wasn't used to people keeping such close tabs on her, and under the circumstances, she was disconcerted.

Philip's onyx cuff links gleamed against the white cuffs of his shirt as he gestured with his hand. "I simply asked Barton where you were when I got home. It's been years since you spent an entire day here, and I was curious."

"Yes, and it's been years since the three of us sat down to dinner together as we are tonight, and Jacey, it's really your fault. If you didn't feel the need to flit around the world so much, this could happen more often. It's almost as if you deliberately stay as far away from us as possible."

"I can't imagine why I'd do a thing like that," Jacey muttered, and rubbed her eyes.

"Well, I for one don't understand it and never have." Edith sighed. "Oh, Philip, I wish your father were here."

"I wouldn't be here if Dad was, as you well know, Edith."

Jacey looked at him and was stunned to see a hint of mischief playing around his lips. It appeared that he had deliberately made a statement that he knew would be guaranteed to draw her mother's fire away from her. It worked.

Edith frowned at him. "Marcus was a good man. Don't be disrespectful to your father's memory, Philip."

"I wasn't aware that I was."

"Well, I know you didn't mean to, but you were, and that attitude is exactly what is wrong with this family."

"Disrespect?"

"No, I meant staying away. You stayed away too long, but at least you came back. Jacey, on the other hand—"

"I think you're mistaken, Edith." He leaned back in his chair, taking his wineglass with him. "I think the thing that's wrong with this family is that we've never been able to get along or agree on anything. But then, from what I hear, that's pretty normal for most families today."

She sent him a stern look, but her tone was gentle. "Whatever the reason, we've been divided too long. Jacey, I'm so glad you've come home. Maybe things can be different now."

"Maybe," she murmured, feeling more of an outsider than ever.

Edith graced her with one of her rare smiles. "I'm so glad you agree."

Agreeing wasn't the problem, she thought ruefully. She had always known it was going to be hard to reconcile with her mother and Philip, she just hadn't fully realized *how* hard until now. After all these years, her mother wasn't going to change. And somehow she couldn't ever imagine herself comfortable enough with Philip to be friends with him.

Edith touched a white linen napkin to either side of her mouth, then placed it beside her plate. "If you're both finished with dinner, why don't you go into the sitting room. Barton will serve coffee, and I'll be along shortly as soon as I have a word with the cook."

Jacey's nerves tensed, and she glanced at Philip. She wasn't ready to be alone with him, but then, she wasn't sure she ever would be.

"Shall we?" he asked.

Excuses formed and reformed in her mind, but none seemed appropriate. Reluctantly she nodded, and before she could push herself away from the table, he was behind her, pulling out her chair.

Two

The sitting room was filled with fine porcelains and paintings, antique mirrors and chests, and fashionably worn brocade sofas and velvet chairs.

And one very large, shaggy-haired dog.

Jacey let out a cry of delight. *"Douglas!"*

The dog lifted his head from the Aubusson rug and happily thumped his tail in greeting.

She dropped down beside him, wrapped her arms around his neck, and buried her face in his fur.

Watching her, Philip decided it was the first truly spontaneous thing he had seen her do in years. She was always so cool, so composed, gazing at him with those extraordinary eyes. They never seemed to warm, but he still remembered a night . . .

"I think he remembers me," she said with a light laugh.

"Why shouldn't he? You're unforgettable."

She glanced up at him. His head was turned as he looked at something across the room, as if he had already forgotten what he had said, but then, she wasn't surprised. He had a history of forgetting. He had managed to forget *her* quite easily.

She stroked Douglas, who had collapsed into a blissful lump by her side. "I'm still amazed every time I see Douglas in the house. It must have taken quite a fight with Mother to get her to agree to letting him stay inside."

His attention returned to her, and his gaze rested on her with a hard brilliance. "It wasn't even a skirmish."

She reconsidered her statement. Philip had left the house when she was eighteen and he was twenty-two, and he hadn't come back until his father had died five years before. When he had returned, he had brought Douglas with him, along with a determination that things would be done his way. And ever since, they had been.

Douglas had momentarily alleviated the tension she felt at being alone with Philip, but now it all came hurtling back. She wished she knew him better, knew what mattered to him, knew what made him happy or sad. He had always seemed larger than life to her, still did in many ways. Maybe if she knew him better, she would be able to put him into some sort of perspective. Maybe.

"Thanks for coming to my aid at dinner. It was nice of you."

He hadn't been able to help himself. Jacey had always given the impression she could deal with her mother's nagging. But tonight she had seemed . . . vulnerable, fragile. His mind was playing tricks on him. "Nice, Jacey? Come on, surely you don't believe that."

She'd like to, but she wasn't sure she did. "Yeah, well, thanks anyway."

"As I said, I was just stating a fact."

Despite his abruptness, her lips moved, curving

slightly upward into a smile. "It reminded me of when I was a teenager. Once in a while back then, you'd do the same thing." She shrugged. "You probably don't remember."

He remembered very well. She had been a colt-ish young girl when she had first come to live there. He had liked her—what was there not to like? She was smart, cute, friendly, and took pains not to intrude on his life. He had treated her like a kid sister, and his father had legally adopted her. A year later he had gone off to college. But when he had come home again that Christmas, he had immediately seen a difference in her. She had seemed more mature, more beautiful, even sexy, and with each succeeding visit she became even more so. Worse, those incredible eyes of hers would stay on him whenever he and she happened to be in the same vicinity, full of longing for something she had known nothing about. And he had begun to experience other feelings, feelings he had done his best to ignore. It had almost worked.

When he didn't say anything, she went on. "I don't know how you've accomplished it, but you've learned to get along with Mother. I suppose I should take lessons."

He shrugged. "It's not so hard. First of all, I feel sorry for her. Since Dad died, she's been very lonely."

She grimaced. "Is that a jab at me for being away all the time?"

His brown eyes held cool assessment. "You're taking things very personally these days, Jacey."

"Only when they are."

Fragile. Very fragile. He shook his head to rid himself of the thought. "Look, you have a right to live any way you see fit. I've certainly never stood in your way."

"No, you haven't. In fact, you turned your back and left."

"What's that supposed to mean?" he asked, and in the next moment silently cursed the sharpness he had been unable to keep from his voice.

She lifted her shoulders and let them fall. "Just what you said. You've never stood in my way."

"I thought we were talking about how I deal with your mother."

"We were. We are." Douglas rolled over on his back and presented his stomach to her. Absently she began scratching him. "Go on."

He exhaled and made a solemn promise to himself that he wasn't going to let her get under his skin. *Not again.* "You have to realize that Edith really does want the best for you. It's just that she can't comprehend that her way isn't the best. Because you're here only on a visit, you're getting her attention in a concentrated form. It's not so bad when it's spread out over weeks and months or even years."

The significance of what he said sank in slowly. "Do you mean to tell me she tries to order you to her liking?"

"Occasionally."

"What do you do?"

"I either ignore her or tell her to stop."

"And she does?"

He nodded, his expression brooding as he watched her. Her hair was in a simple style, the sides pulled back and up and held by two gold combs on either side of her head. The caftan she was wearing was made out of an exotic blue print. He guessed that she had bought it at a bazaar somewhere in the Far East. The garment was relatively shapeless, yet here and there he caught a hint of the curves beneath. She was so damned beautiful, he thought, just as he did every time he saw her. But there was something different about her this time, something more than what could be explained by the fact that he hadn't seen her in three years.

He mentally cursed. What in the hell was he doing? He should be worrying about why she had come home, not about what was different about her. "Giving Edith something else to occupy her mind also works, like planning a dinner party."

"Really? I'm surprised you don't have a string of women friends standing in line to do that for you."

"I didn't say I didn't."

"No, I guess not." Tiny darts of jealousy pricked at her heart, taking her totally by surprise. She should go upstairs, she thought. She was beginning to feel shaky. She gave Douglas a final scratch, gathered her strength, and surged to her feet. The sudden motion sent a wave of dizziness through her, and she lurched toward a chair to grasp its back. Moving so quickly had definitely been a bad idea.

His gaze sharpened. "What's wrong?"

"Nothing. I just lost my balance for a moment."

"That's what you said this morning." He frowned, taking in the fact that she looked even paler than she had a minute before. "You didn't drink at dinner, so you can't be drunk, unless . . . Dammit, Jacey. Are you on drugs?"

She sank onto the couch. "No, Philip, I'm not. But thank you for asking and for your touching faith in me."

"I must have missed something. Is there some reason I should have faith in you?"

Her lips twisted with wry humor. "Well, you've certainly got me there, haven't you? No, I guess I can't think of a reason in the world." She glanced at Douglas and saw that he was gazing mournfully at her for deserting him. She couldn't seem to please anyone in this house, and Philip's next words confirmed it.

"Your mother's right. You are too thin."

Her already frayed nerves unraveled, and she snapped back at him. "And you look tired."

"I've been working long hours lately. What's your excuse?"

"I had a hard time digesting Indian food, that's all."

"Didn't they have a damned McDonald's? Every other country in the world seems to have one."

"I wouldn't know. I didn't look."

"Too busy with your latest admirer? Or should I say admirers?"

In her lap her hands balled into fists. "Would you please tell me *why* I seem to have to keep explaining myself to you and Mother?"

He dropped into a chair at a right angle to her. He loosened his tie, then unbuttoned the top two buttons of his shirt. "Maybe if you stayed around here more so that we could get to know you again, you wouldn't have to."

She looked at him, then away. They were falling right back into the pattern that had taken shape over the past ten years. He would bait her; she would take the hook. She rubbed the spot between her brows. She had had such high hopes when she had lain in that hospital room in Bombay. She had vowed this pattern wouldn't keep repeating itself. She had vowed to find a way to put their past behind them and to go forward. But she had been home only one day and already she was beginning to think she had set herself an impossible task.

"Philip," she said evenly, "do you think we could

carry on a simple, pleasant conversation without any complicated undertones?"

He leaned back and placed an ankle on one knee. "I don't know. For us that would be a fairly innovative concept."

"Are you willing to try?"

Holding her gaze, he slowly nodded his head. "I'd be willing to try anything that would get rid of the knots you've tied in my stomach."

"Me?"

"Most definitely you. The knots have been there ever since I got your fax." And they had tightened when he had first seen her this morning—those long legs, those exotic eyes, that soft mouth. "You see, I can't shake the feeling that you've come home for a reason."

She had wanted to wait to talk to him, but he seemed determined to force the issue. "What if I have?" she asked carefully.

His eyes darkened. "I knew it. You're out to get me, aren't you?"

Her forehead creased in astonishment. She felt as if she had just been hit with a fast ball from left field. "Get you? Philip, what are you talking about? I'm no danger to you."

"Those eyes of yours could freeze a man at twenty paces, but that aside, you're right. You're not a danger to me, at least not personally. I've been inoculated."

He couldn't have said anything more guaranteed to hurt her. Once, ten years before, she had spent the night in his bed. It had been a wondrous, fantastic night, and it and its repercussions had rocked her young life to its foundations. Yet he spoke of the experience as an inoculation.

Douglas got up, ambled over to the side of Philip's chair, and plopped down, unaware and unconcerned with the tension that charged the room.

She should be so lucky, she thought, her fingers automatically going again to the spot between her brows and rubbing. She was fast developing a headache, she realized.

When the virus had first hit her, she had been plagued with a constant, pounding headache that had been almost unbearable. At first the doctors hadn't wanted to give her anything for the pain because they hadn't known what was wrong with her. Lying in that narrow bed, in more pain than she had ever known in her life, she had quickly come to the conclusion that if the unknown disease didn't kill her, the pain surely would. But the doctors had finally prescribed a painkiller, and over the weeks the headache had gradually gone away until now it returned only when she was extremely tired or under stress.

Unfortunately, stressful was the only way to describe her first night at home.

"I don't want any coffee," she murmured. "I'm going up to bed." Before she could move, he was out of his chair and leaning over her, his eyes almost black with intensity. "What the hell kind of game are you playing, Jacey?"

He had placed one hand on the arm of the sofa, the other on its back, penning her. The pounding in her head increased. She had to get upstairs to her room *now*. In another few minutes she would be physically incapable of climbing the stairs. "I'm not playing any game. I don't know—"

"Just tell me one thing. Are you going to ask for your proxy back on the shares that Dad left you?"

"The proxy . . . *That's* what you're afraid of?"

He hit the arm of the sofa with the flat of his hand. "*Tell* me."

She could barely think straight, and so honesty was the easiest, most natural course to take. "Yes."

With a violent shove he jerked upright and took several steps away from her. Every taut line of his body was imbued with a white-hot anger. "Dammit, I know you have every reason to hate me, but I can't believe you're going to do this."

Hate? The word penetrated the haze of pain. Granted, where he was concerned her emotions were confused, but she had never hated him. She was incapable of arguing with him now, though. Slowly, carefully, she stood.

He watched her with narrowed eyes. "I don't have to ask how you found out about what's going on. You have an extensive network of friends, and, of course, Bryan Garry is a particular friend of yours."

Bryan. The name passed swiftly and lightly through her mind, barely making an impression. She headed for the door, concentrating with all her might on putting one foot in front of the other.

His hand snaked out and his fingers clamped around her arm, jerking her to an abrupt halt. She fell against him, and there were agonizing explosions all through her head.

"Dammit, Jacey, I'm not about to let you leave now. Tell me what Bryan has told you. What are their plans? What are yours?"

It was one of the hardest things she had ever had to do, but she forced herself to focus—on his angry face, on the hard line of his mouth, on the dark fire that burned in his eyes. "I . . . haven't . . . spoken . . . to Bryan."

"What—" He broke off and frowned down at her. Something was wrong. "Why are you talking like that?" he asked sharply, then realized that her eyes were dilated to the point that he could see only a thin sliver of aqua circling a huge pool of black. "Dammit, Jacey, you *are* on drugs."

"No—"

"Then what the hell is it? What's wrong with you. Look at me." He smoothed a hand up her forehead to her hair, tilting her head back so that he could examine her more closely.

His touch felt cool and soothing, his body strong and supporting. Her lids slowly lowered as she savored the feelings.

He groaned huskily. "Lord, Jacey, what have you done to yourself?"

Her lids lifted, and she stared up at him. The anger had gone out of him. He seemed troubled about something. "You almost sound as if you care."

"I—"

The door to the sitting room opened and Edith breezed in, a smile wreathing her face. She was carrying a beautiful cut-crystal vase that held two dozen Sterling roses. "Jacey darling, look what just arrived. Do you have any idea who they're from?"

Philip released her so abruptly, she almost fell.

"No," she mumbled. Freed, she turned toward the door.

Edith placed the vase on the coffee table. "Wait, there's a card. Don't you want to read it?"

"No." She had reached the door when she heard Philip speak.

"Give me the card. I'll read it."

Something had made him angry again, she thought vaguely, placing her hand on the door-jamb for support.

"Jacey, I know you'll be interested in this," he said, his voice cutting and hard. "The card says,

'Welcome home. I'll call you tomorrow. Love, Bryan.'"

Jacey didn't know how she made it to and up the stairs. It seemed to take her forever, her agony increasing with each step. At some point she heard the front door slam. Then behind her, in the distance, she heard her mother say, "Jacey, what's Philip so upset about? Where's he going? Where are you going? Jacey?"

She didn't stop, because she knew if she did, she would lose the ability to help herself. And helping herself was very important to her.

Once she reached her room, she headed straight for her purse and the pain pills there. She took two, replaced the pill bottle, and closed the purse, then fell onto the bed and lay absolutely still. Slowly the pain eased, and soon she was claimed by a complete and blissful oblivion.

Philip passed Jacey's bedroom on the way to his and paused outside her room. Light glowed beneath her door. With a scowl he glanced at his watch. One A.M. He had left the house over three hours before and had gone for a drive. He couldn't say where he had been. He also couldn't say that he felt any better. But at least he had his temper back under control.

He stared at the door, hesitating. He had an early morning meeting and probably wouldn't see Jacey before he had to leave for work. But if she were still up, they could finish their talk now. And he had more questions than ever.

He raised his hand and knocked lightly. He waited a minute, and when Jacey didn't open the door, he started to raise his hand again, but then stopped. Edith's bedroom was at the other end of the long hallway, and she was a sound sleeper, but he didn't want to take any chances on waking her. She would only complicate the situation, and heaven knew, there were already enough complications between him and Jacey.

He turned the doorknob and entered the room. "Jacey?"

The crystal lamp on the bedside table was on, the only light in the room. It cast a pale illumination over Jacey, making her skin appear almost colorless. She was lying at an awkward angle across the bed, still wearing the blue caftan and matching flats. The golden combs had fallen from her hair, leaving blond strands in a silky tangle around her head.

He crossed the room to the bed and spoke quietly. "Jacey, wake up."

She didn't stir. He leaned over her and put his hand on her face. She felt cool, *too* cool. He cursed softly. She had obviously been so out of it, she hadn't even been able to undress and get beneath the covers.

Disgusted, he straightened and pivoted for the door. Almost immediately he turned back. She looked as delicate and as breakable as one of her mother's fine porcelains.

With a muttered oath he slipped off her shoes and tossed them on the floor, then he carefully shifted her from one side of the bed to the other so that he could pull the covers down. By the time he was finished, the caftan was twisted up around her knees. Somehow the sight of her bare feet and legs made her appear incredibly defenseless. Feeling like a complete fool for even thinking such a thing, he was nevertheless gentle as he drew the silk down until it was around her ankles, then pulled the covers up over her.

She softly sighed, as if the sudden warmth and comfort were unexpected and she were grateful. The sound bothered the hell out of him.

He went to his room and quickly undressed, then climbed into bed. But sleep eluded him. Instead, memories of that summer ten years earlier came back to him in a rushing flood. And he almost drowned as he remembered.

He had been twenty-two, fresh from college, and bursting with ideas and a need to test them and himself. As a kid he had worked in his father's medical equipment company on school holidays and in the summer. He had begun sweeping floors and had worked himself up through the departments until by the time he had received his degree, there wasn't a machine he couldn't work.

That summer he came home from school full of the arrogance of youth, certain that he knew what was best for the company. The whole plant needed updating, he told his father. To stay a player in the marketplace, a company had to remain one step ahead of its competition. Therefore, all their machinery needed to be updated and replaced. Plus, they badly needed to establish a research and development section.

His father hadn't taken kindly to the suggestions. He had founded the company when he himself was in his twenties and run it successfully ever since. They were doing just fine, and he didn't need some upstart trying to tell him his business, even if the upstart was his own son.

He and his father had argued all summer, the hostilities slowly escalating, until one night it had all come to a head. Words were shouted that were next to impossible to take back, and he had stormed to his room to pack.

Jacey had just graduated from high school, and

was like a flower right before it bursts into full bloom. She had been warm and sympathetic to him, listening for hours as he extolled the virtues of his ideas, encouraging him with her shy smile, unknowingly tempting him just by being.

That night she came to his room. She sat on his bed and tried to calm his anger with soothing words and gentle touches. But he was beyond being calmed. He had had one too many arguments with his father, one too many beers. And she was too damned lovely to ignore any longer.

Full of adrenaline, void of a plan, he had pulled her to him and kissed her. And her sweetness was his complete undoing.

She was innocent, but she didn't resist. She folded her arms around his neck, and beneath his hands and mouth she came alive until suddenly he was holding pure fire.

Her young body accepted him again and again that night. It was beyond him to leave her alone. She was everything he wanted and more. Finally, toward dawn, they fell into an exhausted sleep, entangled in each other's arms.

In the night she had been all giving, all red-hot heat. But the cold light of day had come too soon, and he had never seen her that way again. Try as he might, though, he had never been able to forget the fire of that night.

And now she was back. To ruin him.

Three

"So you've finally decided to emerge from your room," Edith said that afternoon as she ensconced herself on the cushioned, outdoor lounge chair next to Jacey's and carefully arranged the skirt of her dress over her legs.

Jacey smiled, but chose not to respond to her mother's irritated tone. "I couldn't resist coming out here. It's such a lovely afternoon, isn't it?" The lounge chairs were set up at the back of the house on a manicured lawn that stretched expansively down to the Hudson. Sunlight sparkled on the water and warmed her face. Douglas lay on the ground at her feet, napping. She felt good; her headache was completely gone.

"Yes, and it was a lovely *morning* too. I don't understand why you insisted on staying in your room so long. I sent the maid to your room at eight to see if you wanted to join me for breakfast."

"Yes, I know." The maid had awakened her from a deep sleep with the message. She had declined. Deciding to play it safe and take it easy, she had dozed away most of the morning. At noon she had eaten a leisurely lunch in her room, and then ventured outside to get some fresh air. "Look at the trees. The colors of the leaves are breathtaking, aren't they?"

With obvious reluctance Edith glanced around her. "Marcus loved the fall. I have always preferred spring, when things slowly come to bloom, but he liked the brisk energy of fall." A small smile touched her lips. "But then, he was such a dynamic man."

He was also a stubborn man with a great deal of pride, Jacey reflected. Like his son. Being too much alike was the main reason Marcus and Philip hadn't gotten along.

Edith cleared her throat as if it would help clear her mind and allow her to get back to the present. "What exactly went on last night, Jacey?"

"I'm not sure what you're talking about." It was true. Once the headache hit her, events had blurred until she couldn't remember too much. Except she did remember that Philip had been very angry with her about something.

"It was my understanding that we were all going to have coffee together. The next thing I knew, you went upstairs and Philip left the house. It was most odd."

Her mother sounded so bewildered, Jacey couldn't help but feel sorry for her. "Well, I can account for my behavior. I was simply tired and decided to go to bed early."

Edith studied her daughter with a frown. "I'm glad you've decided to stay home for a while. It's obvious that all the traveling has taken a toll."

"Yes," she murmured, "I guess it has."

Edith's frown deepened. "I wonder what was wrong with Philip."

In an effort to minimize her own uneasiness

over the same question, Jacey shrugged. "Does there need to be something wrong with him? When I was living here, I remember many a night when he left the house and didn't come back until dawn."

"He's changed, Jacey. He's no longer the young hothead he was, and he's been very good to me, allowing me to stay on after Marcus's death. After all, the house is his now."

"I'm sure it's a big help to him to have you to run things for him."

Edith's manicured hands fluttered restlessly in her lap. "I don't do that much. The household staff is excellent. Eventually, I'll have to find my own place, not that it will be a problem. Marcus left me well provided for in other ways, as he did you. But one of these days I'm sure Philip will want to marry and start his own family. I mean, it's just natural that he will, isn't it?"

Her mother's rhetorical question touched a nerve in Jacey. "Is there someone special in his life now?" she asked slowly.

"No. At least I don't think there is. Lately he seems to spend all his time at work, too much time, if you ask me."

So there could be someone in his life, she thought. In fact, she would be surprised if there weren't. Her mother was right. It was natural that he find someone. That summer night the two of them had shared had been so long ago. They owed each other nothing.

"Wasn't it nice of Bryan Garry to send you the roses? They're really exquisite."

"Roses?" Jacey asked blankly.

"The Sterling roses." Her mother looked at her curiously. "Have you forgotten? They were delivered right before you went upstairs."

Now that she thought about it, she did have a vague memory of someone saying something about roses. And about Bryan. "I guess I did forget."

"Well, it was very nice of him to send them to welcome you home. I didn't realize the two of you were so close."

Bryan was her age and they had gone to school together. They had run around in the same group, going to movies and attending school functions. They had even had a real date once, but had quickly fallen back into the more familiar and convenient pattern of friendship. "We've always been good friends, you know that."

"I guess I'd forgotten. You've been gone so long."

Jacey grimaced, but remained silent.

"How did he know you were home?"

"I ran into Sara Blackman at the airport as I was coming in. She was returning from London. She probably spread the news."

"Mrs. Killane?"

Edith glanced around at Barton. "Yes?"

"Mr. Gage is here to see you."

Edith's hand flew to her breast. "Oh, dear, what do you suppose he wants?" The question was directed to herself rather than to either Jacey or Barton.

"Who's Mr. Gage?" Jacey asked.

"Robert Gage. You don't know him, darling. He's from Oklahoma, but just in the past few years he's expanded his business interests to New York and New Jersey. And for some reason, someone happened to bring him to our club one day, and I guess he decided he liked it, because he applied for membership. Now it seems as if I bump into him everywhere I go."

"Shall I tell him you'll be in directly?" Barton

inquired in his neutral butler's voice that betrayed nothing of what he might be thinking about the people who employed him and the events that surrounded them.

But Jacey happened to be looking at him as he was speaking and was surprised to see a twinkle in his eyes.

"What? Oh, yes, do that, Barton. And put him in the solarium. There aren't any porcelains in there for him to break."

"Yes, Mrs. Killane."

"Mr. Gage breaks your porcelain?" Jacey asked curiously as Barton turned back to the house.

"No, he never has, but I expect him to every time he comes. He's such a big man, and he's so . . . full of life." She glanced after Barton, her expression apprehensive. "Well, I guess there's nothing for me to do but to go see what he wants. He probably got wind of our latest charity event and wants to help."

"You sound as if you don't like him, but if he came here to offer help, he must be a nice man."

"Yes, well, I suppose he is. He's just so . . ." She cleared her throat. "I don't know. Did I tell you he's from Oklahoma?"

"Yes, you did. Is that significant in some way?"

"What? Oh. I guess not. You know, I've never been to Oklahoma. I don't think I even know anyone who's been there, and now here this man is and he's from there, and . . . well, I've just never met anyone like him before, that's all."

After Edith left, Jacey settled back into the cushioned lounger to enjoy the rest of the afternoon. Despite her mother's obvious reluctance to see this Mr. Gage, Jacey had no doubt that she would be able to handle the man's unexpected visit.

It was a cool but sunny day, with a light breeze that every once in a while sent red-, gold-, and orange-patterned leaves cartwheeling across the lawn. She had dressed in jeans and boots and attempted to hide her weight loss with an oversize, thick-weaved fisherman's sweater that fell to the middle of her thighs.

Physically and emotionally, yesterday had been hard on her, but today she felt better, even a little stronger. And the conversation she had just had with her mother hadn't been too bad. Perhaps things would work out as she wanted them to after all.

"Hello, Jacey."

Her nerves jumped at the sound of Philip's voice. Maybe, she thought with wry humor, she had been too optimistic in her forecast. She looked up at him, at the same time raising her hand to shield her eyes from the sun. "Philip. Isn't it a little early for you to be home?"

He dropped down on the lounger beside her, facing her, his feet planted firmly on the ground. Douglas levered his bulk to his feet and ambled over to him. Philip obligingly scratched him behind the ears, but his attention never once wavered from her.

"I have to go back in a few minutes. I just came home to check on you."

"Me?" she asked, startled.

Sensing his master's interest had been diverted, Douglas plopped down beside him.

Philip nodded. He hadn't been able to get her out of his mind all day. He had almost convinced himself he was wrong about thinking that she was on drugs. There had to be some other explanation for her behavior. She was too smart to be involved in such self-destructive behavior. Wasn't she?

He had asked himself the question over and over, but in the end he had finally had to face the truth. He saw her so seldom, he had no idea what she could be involved in or with whom. And as inconvenient and downright annoying as he found it, he hadn't been able to stop himself from worrying. "How are you?"

"I'm fine."

She did look much better, he thought, relieved. Her skin seemed to have more color, and her eyes were back to their normal, infinitely fascinating, icy aqua.

She shifted uneasily beneath the intensity of his stare. He was wearing a navy blue suit paired with a blue shirt and a patterned silk tie. As always, he looked formidable and incredibly attractive. She could even smell his cologne, a heady combination of citrus and masculinity. She searched her mind for something to say. "I—"

"What was wrong with you last night?"

Automatically she used the explanation she had given her mother. "I was tired."

He shook his head. "No, it was more than that. You were speaking strangely, and your eyes were dilated. You even seemed to have trouble maintaining your balance."

She gave an inner sigh. She supposed letting him in on part of the truth wouldn't hurt anything. "I had a headache."

"It must have been a bad one."

"It was."

"Why the hell didn't you tell me?"

"I didn't want to make a big deal out of it."

"Yeah, but I could have gotten you something for it."

"I had something in my room. As soon as I got up there, I took it and went to sleep."

His gaze turned brooding as he remembered the deep sleep he had found her in. "Do you get headaches often?"

"No." Not anymore.

He reached for her hand and intently searched her face. "Jacey, would you tell me if you were in any kind of trouble?"

She was trying to adjust to the surprising fact that he had taken her hand; the dismaying question made her task even harder.

"Would you?" he pressed.

She considered his question and again decided she could only be honest. "Probably not," she said, then hurried to add, "but, Philip, I'm not in any trouble."

He smiled crookedly. "You just got through saying you wouldn't tell me."

She drew a deep breath. "Last night you were angry with me. Today you seem concerned. I've told you I had a headache but that I'm fine now. I don't understand what it is you want from me."

Damn good point, he thought grimly. She had admitted she wanted her proxy back, the very thing he had feared. They'd have to talk about it and soon. Her votes were critical to him and KillaneTech. But having her home for this extended length of time was bringing back all sorts of memories and emotions with a force and power he wouldn't have thought possible. At a time when he didn't need to be distracted, he most definitely was.

He gazed down at the hand he held. It was small and delicate, with tapered fingers that held no rings and nails that were painted crimson. He could still remember the way her hands had felt as they stroked his body. Sometimes he thought he would give all he possessed to erase that one night from his memory.

She watched him, trying unsuccessfully to decipher his expression. It was hard for her to distance herself from him so that she could be objective and see him as a person rather than as a man with a pure and potent maleness about him who could send her blood pressure skyrocketing.

Last night he had been angry with her; today he appeared to be reaching out to her in some way. Though she didn't understand why, it was more than she had hoped for. She sat up and swung her legs over the side of the lounger so that she faced him. The change of position brought her so close to him, she had to shift her legs so that their knees wouldn't touch. Impulsively, she laid her hand on top of his. "Thank you for being concerned, Philip, but I'm fine. I really am."

He lifted his gaze from her hands to her eyes. "Let me ask you another question. Would you tell me if you were on drugs?"

"Drugs?" She recoiled, pulling her hands from his. "Lord, Philip, you accused me of being on drugs last night, didn't you?"

"The way you were acting—"

"I had a *headache*."

His eyes narrowed. "I hope you did, Jacey, because I would hate to think you've gotten involved with anything as stupid and guaranteed to mess up your life as drugs."

"I had a headache," she repeated firmly.

"Okay, fine."

Her indignation over the fact that he would think she was capable of such a thing slowly turned to curiosity. "Did you really come home just because you were worried about me?"

His lips twisted. "Do you find it so hard to

believe that I'm capable of being concerned about someone else?"

"No. Well, that is, I guess I do when that someone is me."

"No matter what, Jacey, you're family."

She tore her gaze from his and looked away. "Yes, I guess I am."

Maybe it was the fact that he was so happy to see that she was better. Maybe it was the glasslike fragility he still sensed about her. Maybe it was the fact that she had put her hand on his of her own accord. Or maybe it was just because he was so close to her. But suddenly he wanted her to look at him again. He skimmed his fingers along her jawline and with gentle pressure turned her so that she was forced to look at him. And he was completely taken off guard by the shadows he saw clouding her eyes.

"What's wrong, Jacey?" he asked softly. "You can tell me."

Warmth lingered where he had touched. Feelings, new and, at the same time, old, mixed and built inside her. "Nothing. Why do you ask?"

"There's something different about you. . . ."

Striving for a casualness she didn't feel, she shrugged. "It's been three years. There's bound to be a few things different about me."

"It's more than that—" He stopped, and an indecipherable sound rose from his chest. "Sweet heaven, those eyes of yours have always had the ability to tear right through me."

She wasn't sure what was happening, but she felt as if the ground had suddenly tilted beneath her. With an instinctive, desperate need to right it, she said, "Look, I think we need to talk."

"Yes, you're right, we do. . . ." The words came out on a husky whisper.

Unwillingly, her gaze dropped to his lips. They were full, firm, and capable of producing an extraordinary fire in her. She had had only that one night with him. He had never touched her in any intimate way before or since. But the memory still burned in her. Oh, how the memory burned. . . .

She swayed forward, and his hands encircled her arms. He had no idea what he was going to do or say right up to the second he opened his mouth. "Tell me you don't hate me."

The dark fire in his eyes mesmerized her. "Hate? No, I don't, and . . . I don't. I don't think I ever have."

The fires burned higher. "Tell me you didn't come home to hurt me."

A vaguely disquieting voice deep inside her told her something wasn't right. His tone carried an unusual fierceness. Hurt him? What was he talking about? "I didn't. Why would I—"

He leaned forward and pressed his mouth to hers. The contact shattered every sane thought, and suddenly she was totally caught up in the feel of his lips on hers. They were hard and hot, and there was nothing or no one else in the world but Philip and her on this sun-filled afternoon. Her hand lifted to rest along the side of his face, and she felt the muscles in his jaw work as he thrust his tongue deep into her mouth. An electric pleasure jolted through her from the top of her head to the tips of her toes.

She was surprised at how familiar his taste was to her, at how well known the texture of his hair was as she slid her fingers through it, at how at home his tongue was in her mouth. She tangled her tongue with his; the velvet scraping caused warmth to flash, then settle in the pit of her stomach.

His hands tightened around her arms, and he pulled her closer to him until she was perched on the very edge of her lounger. Then one hand left her arm and went to the soft skin of her neck.

"Dammit, this shouldn't be happening," he murmured even as his mouth devoured her hungrily.

Somehow her cobweb-filled mind grasped the meaning of what he said, and agreed. He was absolutely right. What they were doing made no sense. But she made no move to pull away. She felt as if she were in a fevered dream, one like the many she had had when she had been so sick. He had been in those dreams, she realized, a hard, angry man with a passion that overwhelmed her.

And then, as now, there was a sound, an intrusion that parted the clouds of her dream.

"Miss Killane?" Barton discreetly cleared his throat. "I'm sorry to bother you, but there's a call."

With a rough sound Philip jerked away from her and glared up at the butler. "What in the hell is it?"

"I'm sorry, sir, but Mr. Bryan Garry is on the phone for Miss Killane. I told him she was busy, but he insisted that it was important."

Dazed, Jacey saw Barton tilt his head back and stare up at the sky, examining the fluffy white clouds as if trying to decide if they needed tidying into a more uniform formation.

Philip surged up and away from the lounger. Several feet away, he stopped with his back to her and shoved his hands into his trouser pockets.

Barton handed her the portable phone, then quietly retreated to the house.

Jacey couldn't tear her gaze away from Philip. He looked so remote, so distant, when only seconds before . . .

"Jacey? Jacey, are you there?"

She heard Bryan's voice and lifted the phone to her ear. "Yes, Bryan, I'm here."

"Great. I thought I'd never get Barton to put me through. How are you? Welcome home! Did you get my roses?"

Bryan sounded just as he always had, she thought with a rush of gratitude and affection. Friendly, uncomplicated, and happy. At least that one thing in the world hadn't changed. The knowledge helped her to slowly regain her composure. "Roses? Yes, I did. Thank you very much. They're lovely." She couldn't remember actually seeing them, but they had to be lovely. Bryan wouldn't have sent anything less.

"Good. I was really excited when Sara told me you were back. It's been too long since any of us have seen you."

"I agree." She stared at Philip's back and didn't have to see his face to know that once again he was very angry with her. Making him angry had to be a special talent she had. "Listen, Bryan, could I call you back in a little while?"

"Oh, I'm sorry. Did I catch you at a bad time?"

She eyed the rigidity of Philip's spine. "Sort of."

"Okay, then, I'll let you go. But first tell me you'll have lunch with me."

"Lunch? When?" she asked, her mind on Philip. He had suddenly gone even more rigid.

"When's good for you? Tomorrow?"

"No."

"How about the next day?"

Something clicked in her brain. She had made a doctor's appointment for Thursday. "Uh . . . what day is that?"

"Thursday."

"Thursday will be great." She would be in the

city anyway, and she could kill two birds with one stone. "I'll call you later, and we can decide on where."

"Great. Talk to you soon."

"Soon," she agreed. "Bye." She pushed the button to disconnect the phone.

Philip slowly turned. "If you and Bryan had things to talk about that you didn't want me to hear, all you had to do was ask me to leave. Not that I would have, but it might have been worth a try."

Tossing the phone aside, she stood and eyed him steadily. "If Bryan and I had things to talk about, calling him back later would have served the same purpose. But that wasn't the case."

"Yet you told him you'd call him back."

"Yes. Because . . . I felt it was more important that you and I talk now. I mean, his call . . . interrupted us. What just happened between us was . . . a surprise. . . ."

"I apologize. It won't happen again."

She took a moment to absorb that, and decided that there was nothing more ego deflating than having a man kiss you, then apologize. "Plus, I could tell that you were angry again."

"Again?"

"You were angry last night."

"I tend to become angry when someone tries to take something away from me that's mine."

Her brows drew together. "What on earth are you talking about? Who's trying to take what away from you?"

His lips curved into a smile that was hard enough to cut a diamond. He stepped to her and lightly grazed his fingers down one cheek. "Look at you. Butter wouldn't melt in your mouth. I was actually worried about you, and when you said you didn't come home to hurt me, I swallowed it hook, line, and sinker." He gave a short laugh. "I guess my only excuse is that I wanted so damned much to believe you."

She gritted her teeth. "I didn't come home to hurt you, and I repeat. Who and what are you talking about?"

"You and Bryan, sweetheart. Who else? Who else but you has reason to hate me? But I've got to say, I like the way you kiss when you hate." He reached out to her again, this time rubbing his thumb across her lips with an almost painful pressure. "I take it all back," he said roughly. "It will happen again. Why not? I might as well get something out of this deal." He paused, his expression cruel. "You were good when you were eighteen. You must be twice as good now."

Her head swam. He had jumped from a subject she didn't know to one she knew very well. She felt heat staining her cheeks. "You bastard."

His eyebrows arched. "What's the matter? Do you think bringing up our past is hitting below the belt? That's nothing compared to what you and Bryan plan. Besides, admit it. Our past is there between us whether we want it to be or not. We might as well use it to our mutual benefit."

"Philip, I don't un—"

"It's hell, isn't it? Being slapped in the face with your own weapon. But relax. You'll like it. I guarantee it. Having sex with the enemy will add excitement to the whole thing."

She had to stop whatever was happening, because whatever it was, it was wrong. "*No. Nothing's* going to happen between us. Not now. Now ever."

He leaned down and pressed a hard, hurting kiss to her lips. "I have to get back to the office. Don't lock your door tonight."

Four

Jacey had no intention of locking her door. She was determined to wait up for Philip. Her emotions ranged from anger to indignation to utter embarrassment. He definitely owed her some answers and she was going to have them. But by eleven that night he still hadn't returned home, and she fell asleep. When she woke up at nine the next morning, he was gone again.

Her first impulse was to drive to his office and demand an explanation, but she forced herself to calm down and look rationally at the situation. First of all, she wasn't sure how her strength would hold up to the drive and then what was sure to be an emotional encounter. Considering the circumstances, she didn't want to put herself to the test. Next, obviously there was something going on that she needed to know about. But it only stood to reason that if whatever was going on involved her, she would eventually find out what it was. In the meantime, she had no intention of giving Philip the satisfaction of running after him.

Their kiss had left her badly shaken. It illustrated clearly how easily he could make her respond to him. *Still*. After *ten* years.

She would like to think that she could chalk up her lack of resistance to him to the weakened state of her health, but deep down inside she wasn't sure she could. For one thing, she was feeling better every day. For another, she had the awful suspicion that Philip would be able to raise her from the dead simply by touching his lips to hers.

But it didn't matter, she told herself firmly. She had no intention of dying anytime soon. And next time, if there was a next time, she would be much stronger and therefore more in control.

To that end and to her mother's consternation, she spent the entire day resting. She managed to ignore the pointed remarks and even had a couple of almost-pleasant conversations with her. She ate well and napped, and when Philip didn't come home for dinner, she went to bed early. And she wasn't surprised or displeased to find that when she woke the next morning, he once again had left.

Having previously arranged for a car and driver for the day, she had breakfast in her room. She chose a comfortable, long brown suede skirt with matching jacket, low-heeled boots, and a long jade-green cashmere sweater. She didn't feel like bothering with jewelry, but she took a jade silk scarf and tied her hair low on her neck.

Once she was dressed, she took a moment to study herself in the mirror. The purple smudges beneath her eyes were fading, but . . . She raised her fingers to her mouth. Was it only her imagination that made her think her lips were still swollen from Philip's hard kisses? It had to be.

Just before ten Edith knocked on her door and

walked in. "Darling, there's a car waiting down-stairs for you. Where are you going?"

With a smile she scooped up her purse and draped its gold chain strap over her shoulder. "Good morning, Mother. I'm going into the city to run a few errands and have lunch with Bryan. I should be back for dinner, though."

Edith's perplexed expression cleared. "A few hours in the city sounds like fun. I was beginning to wonder about you. You've done nothing but rest since you've been home. You haven't acted like yourself at all."

Her lips twisted with wry humor. "What's the matter? Don't you like spending time alone with me?"

"Why, of course I do, but—"

She crossed the room and pressed a kiss to her mother's cheek. "My latest travels have just left me a little tired, that's all. I'll see you tonight."

Three hours later, after a successful trip to the doctor, she was greeting Bryan in the lobby of a trendy restaurant on the Upper East Side.

"You're a sight for sore eyes, young lady," Bryan said with a grin after they were seated. "I saw you in Paris last spring, but then I lost track of you."

She smiled. "Well, I'm here now, and it's great to see you too." She was in a tremendously good mood. After reviewing her medical records from India, the doctor had drawn blood and told her he would have the results in a couple of days. But his preliminary examination showed what she already felt, that she was well on the road to recovery. And Bryan was a genuinely nice man, not to mention good company. It was too bad that she had never fallen in love with him—her life would be so simple and pleasant if she had. But then, she reflected ruefully, she had never been able to fall in love with anyone. "By the way, thank you again for the roses."

"My pleasure."

They paused to place their orders, then set out to catch up on news of old acquaintances.

"Bryan," Jacey said slowly nearly an hour later as she finished eating. "Have you had any dealings with Philip lately? He became very upset when you called."

Bryan threw back head and laughed with delight. "I can't believe it. You mean I actually managed to ruffle the feathers of the great Philip Killane? I didn't think anyone or anything could do that."

"Well, you did, and then some. He accused me of working with you on something. Do you know what he's talking about?"

He laughed again, his delight increasing. "As a matter of fact, I do. My dad's company is making a run on KillaneTech. I work for my dad. You and I are friends. You hold a great deal of the stock. Looks like Philip added two and two and got twenty-two."

Her proxy. He had asked her if she planned on taking it back. Lord, how could she have forgotten that? "You mean the company is in trouble?"

He shrugged. "I guess it depends on your viewpoint, but KillaneTech is definitely vulnerable at the moment. Philip has recently spent a lot of money on new machinery, which has left the company relatively cash poor. It's an excellent opportunity for Dad and me." His gaze turned thoughtful. "To tell you the truth, Jacey, it never occurred to me that you would throw your vote our way, and frankly I'm surprised Philip thought you would. He doesn't know you very well, does he?"

She shook her head thoughtfully. "No, he doesn't, and frankly, I'm beginning to wonder if it's possible that he ever will."

She arrived back at the house at three, and since the trip into the city had left her tired, she took a long nap. When she awoke, it was already dark. Feeling completely rested, she took a bath and dressed for dinner. She chose a cream silk chiffon shirtwaist dress that had a pleated bodice and a softly gathered long skirt.

"You look lovely, darling," her mother said when she saw her, "but you still look too thin."

"How strange," Jacey said mildly. "I'm actually gaining weight."

They dined alone, and Jacey refused to allow Philip's nonappearance to upset her. She was ready to confront him, and she had a feeling it would be soon. Until then, she was content to bide her time.

She and her mother were in the sitting room having coffee when they heard Philip come home and go directly to his study. Jacey waited for him to join them, but after some time had passed and he hadn't, she rose.

"I think I'll take a cup of coffee in to Philip."

Her mother smiled. "That would be nice, dear. I'm sure he'll appreciate it. Tell him good night for me, will you? I think I'll go up and finish a book I'm reading."

Philip leaned his head against the back of his desk chair and closed his eyes. These past two days he had driven himself until he was nearly exhausted, and his nerves were strung to the snapping point. He should have taken it a little easier, but he hadn't been able to make himself. Jacey was too much on his mind and work had been a way to try to escape her.

He had lashed out in anger at her and threatened sexual reprisals. He had been a complete jerk to do it, and he knew it. But the truth was, he hadn't trusted himself to come home. He had stayed away because he was afraid that he might do exactly what he had threatened. But not because of any retaliation or anger.

Something had happened to him since she had returned. The few times he had seen her in the last ten years, she had seemed remote and untouchable. But now, at the single most crucial point of his career, she suddenly seemed soft and warm and very, very touchable. And no matter how many meetings he had, no matter how many reports he studied, he couldn't stop thinking about her.

The door opened, and Jacey walked in, wearing a dress that flowed caressingly against her body, emphasizing the curves beneath the soft, sensual material as she crossed the room to his desk. He wondered if she knew how much he would like to be inside her, pumping in and out, until they both exploded with a mind-blowing, soul-destroying pleasure. He briefly closed his eyes against the image and the feelings that were suddenly very real to him. Lord help him. He had lied when he had told her she wasn't a danger to him personally.

As she drew nearer, Jacey saw him close his eyes, as if he didn't want to see her. Trying not to let it upset her, she sought a diversion. For a few brief moments she forcibly cast her mind back to when Marcus had occupied the study. It was an imposing room, and Marcus had been just as imposing. But whenever she had ventured in and found Marcus sitting behind that very desk, he would always put aside what he was working on and talk to her about whatever it was that happened to be troubling her. And she would always leave feeling better.

Wordlessly, she leaned forward and placed the cup of steaming coffee in front of Philip. After all the years, the study was still imposing, and Philip looked as if he belonged. Somehow, though, she didn't think she would leave feeling better. She sat down.

He looked at her assessingly. "Thank you for the coffee, but there's no reason for you to stay."

"I think there is," she said, crossing her legs. He was in his shirt-sleeves, with the cuffs folded back. Fine, silky, dark hair covered his strong forearms. She knew that a mat of similarly textured hair covered his chest. And lower on his body . . . A faint tingle of heat crept up her spine.

"Look, I'm too tired to argue with you tonight."

"Good, it's time we stopped arguing and talked, *really* talked."

He kept his head against the back of the chair and studied her with narrowed eyes. She was all cream, ivory, and gold—and cool, very cool, like a calla lily on a frosty morning. As tired and worried as he was, he couldn't shake the urge to set a fire simmering in her blood with kisses and caresses until the frost that surrounded her melted. He was losing his mind. He should get up and walk out before he gave in to his impulse, he thought. He stayed where he was.

"Okay, Jacey, what subject would you like to talk about?" he asked, but then held up his hand, stopping her from answering. "Let me guess. You had lunch with Bryan today, didn't you?"

"Yes, I did."

"Then I would guess this little talk you propose we have has to do with him and his father's company, plus, of course, KillaneTech." He spread his hands out. "How did I do?"

"You're very clever, as always, Philip."

"Thank you. How was the lunch anyway? Did he take you to a nice place?"

"Yes, he did, and our lunch was fun."

"Really? Fun? My idea of fun would be if Bryan choked on a piece of meat." His expression turned mockingly hopeful. "I don't suppose that happened?"

"No."

"Pity."

She eyed him thoughtfully. "And even if he had, I know the Heimlich maneuver."

"It figures."

"The lunch was also illuminating. I learned a lot."

"I'll just bet you did." Suddenly he propelled himself forward and propped his elbows on the arm of the chair. "So what do you want, Jacey? A pound of flesh? A pint of blood? My company?"

"What I'd like," she said carefully, "is a lucid, rational conversation, where we lay all the cards on the table."

He folded his hands across his abdomen. "I don't see anything wrong with that. What cards are you holding, Jacey?"

"None."

"It doesn't look like that from where I'm sitting. In fact, it looks to me as if you're holding a hand that's going to be damned hard to beat. Too bad I'm not going down without a fight."

She sighed. She felt as if she were trying to handle a riled porcupine. There wasn't a chance in the world she could do it without getting hurt. "Okay, let's back up a little. The first night I was home, you asked me if I was going to take back my proxy. I said yes."

"That you did. In fact, I'm surprised you haven't already presented me with the proper notice in triplicate."

Seeing the doctor and Bryan had been all she had been able to manage in one day. She hadn't felt up to meeting with her lawyer too, but she had made the appointment. "I'll have the documentation in a few days. Until then, I want you to understand why I am revoking the proxy."

"I already know."

"No. You *think* you know, but the truth is, you don't have a clue." She rushed on before he could speak. "It's not entirely your fault that you don't. I'm aware that I haven't exactly been the easiest person in the world to get in touch with these last few months."

"No one can make an understatement quite like you, Jacey."

She gritted her teeth and smiled sweetly. "Thank you." She had had long hours to think in that lonely, faraway hospital room, and one of the resolutions she had made was that it was time to take charge of her life and to gear it in a productive direction. "Getting back to the subject at hand, I'm revoking the proxy because I think I've had a free ride long enough. The truth is, I've left the responsibility of my shares up to you for far too long. I want to shoulder my portion of the burden now."

"How virtuous. How considerate. How totally suspect."

She eyed him calmly. "You've tried me and found me guilty before hearing any evidence at all."

"I wouldn't throw stones. I remember a time when you did the same thing to me." He pushed up from the chair and walked to a window. The heavy brocade drapes hadn't been drawn yet, and outside, the night was ink black. No matter how hard he tried, he couldn't penetrate the blackness.

She shifted in the chair. "I think we'll do better if we leave our history out of this."

"Fine, we can try that if you like." He wheeled back to the mahogany desk, placed his hands on its gleaming surface, and leaned toward her. "Let's talk present. Right now, as we speak, there are people trying for my jugular, Jacey. You'll forgive me if I feel somewhat self-protective."

The temptation was great, but she never dropped her gaze from his. "I didn't know, Philip. I swear to you I knew nothing of what has been going on with KillaneTech until Bryan told me today at lunch."

The hell of it was he wanted to believe her. He wanted to believe her so much, he hurt with the need. He dropped wearily back into the chair. "You and Bryan? What about the two of you?"

"We're just good friends. We've been good friends since junior high. And guess what? We're such good friends and know each other so well, he said it never even occurred to him that I would throw my vote to him."

"And you believed him?"

"He doesn't have a devious bone in his body."

"And I gather you expect me to believe the same of you?"

Her self-possession was beginning to come at a higher and higher price. She could feel her nerves beginning to fray and her muscles protesting because she was holding herself so stiffly. "Frankly I couldn't care less what you do or don't believe, but what I do want, expect, in fact *demand*, is for you to do me—as a major stockholder in KillaneTech—the courtesy of telling me exactly what is going on."

Sweet heaven. She seemed as cool and remote as the moon that hung somewhere out in the night sky, infinitely more desirable, and equally unattainable. How in the hell could he concentrate on the problems of his company when his body ached for release inside her? The simple answer was he had to.

He straightened and raked a hand through his hair. "All right. Here it is. The company was in a bad way when I took over five years ago after Dad's death. He had let things slip. Almost immediately I began to systematically get rid of the antiquated machinery that Dad had put such faith in for so many years and replace it with state-of-the-art machinery."

She nodded that she understood while her mind raced back ten years to that night. Insisting that the machinery needed to be replaced had been what had led to that final, fateful blowup with Marcus. It had ended with Philip moving out. But first she had gone to his room and spent the night.

"I've tried to replace it slowly, taking a division at a time. But even doing it that way has been an enormous drain on the company's capital. Still, we would have been all right, except a few months ago, the remaining machinery began breaking down. It got so bad we weren't even meeting our quota." He grimaced. "And it came at a hell of a time. I was right in the middle of trying to negotiate new contracts." He shrugged. "I had no choice but to bite the bullet and replace the remaining equipment in one fell swoop. Of course, purchasing and installation doesn't happen overnight. It's taken time, and for a while we were running at only about forty percent capacity. Now we're nearly back to normal, but it's left us with barely any cash flow and the proud possessor of a nice size business loan." He smiled without humor. "That's the good news."

"And the bad?"

"The companies with whom I was negotiating have put their contracts on temporary hold. First they want to make sure the company is stable enough that I can deliver what I say I can. Second, they, like Bryan and his father, have smelled blood, and they're waiting to see who they're going to be dealing with before they grant those contracts."

"Are any stockholders selling?"

"So far only one or two minor holders have, but my guess is that the others will follow soon. The news of the Garrys' interest is out, and the value of the stock is slowly climbing. There's a waiting game going on to see how high it will climb, but they're going to wait only so long."

She thought for a minute. He had thirty percent of the stock, and she had fifteen. Even taking into account that he had to answer to the board of directors, he would have an enormous advantage and would represent a majority block if he had the ability to vote her stock. Without it, he was in serious trouble.

He seemed to read her mind. "My old man was a

piece of work, wasn't he? Even in death he couldn't stand to see me running the show."

"I was as surprised as you when he left me the stock. You know that."

He abruptly sliced a hand through the air. "I don't begrudge you the income, Jacey. I never have. But I badly need the leverage your stock will give me. Can I keep the proxy?"

She stared back at him, delaying for several moments her answer. She didn't need to hear the urgency that was in his voice to know how important the company was to him. And she finally understood his anger. Even as a teenager he had loved KillaneTech. He had cared enough about the company to leave when his father wouldn't do what he thought was right for it. And he had cared enough to come back, even though by that time he had established a growing company of his own.

But she also remembered how near death she had been just a couple of months before and the resolves that had come out of that experience. He wouldn't understand how important those resolves were to her. Perhaps no one would. But they had been at the very heart of her determination to get well. "No."

With a muttered oath he flung himself back in the chair. "Dammit, Jacey—"

"Listen to me. I didn't say I would vote against you. I said only that I want to control my own votes. It's one of the reasons I came home."

He wiped a hand across his face, then looked at her, his expression grim. "So how long are you going to keep me hanging?"

"I'll come to the plant tomorrow afternoon, and you can show me what you've done and explain in detail exactly what the company is up against.

Then I'll decide." She pushed herself up from the chair and started for the door.

His fear about her taking back her proxy had proved to be square on the mark, he thought, and the urge to wring her beautiful neck was strong. But he couldn't shake the sense that there was something else she hadn't told him. He supposed he shouldn't give a damn, but . . . "Jacey?"

She turned. "Yes?"

"You said revoking your proxy was *one* of the reasons you came home. What is the other?"

"I had several reasons," she said, hedging.

"I see." He paused. "Do any of these reasons concern me? Because if they do, I'd like to know right now."

She hesitated. She could tell herself that they had enough between them to resolve for now, and she would be right. But there was one more thing he had a right to know. One more thing he *should* know.

She squared her shoulders, then returned to stand behind the chair she had been sitting in and rested her hands on its high back. She was about to need its support.

"There is something that I meant to tell you sooner, but things kept getting in the way."

"What is it?"

"I came home to give you a divorce."

Five

Philip stilled. "Would you mind repeating that?"

She dug her fingers into the nubby-weave upholstery of the chair. "You didn't misunderstand me. One of the reasons I came home was to give you a divorce."

His jaw clenched. "I thought we *were* divorced. In fact, I distinctly remember you flying off to Mexico the day after you graduated from college to get the divorce. You said it was your graduation present to yourself."

She was beginning to feel tired, but she wasn't sure if the cause was physical or emotional. Heaven knew, she had been dreading having to tell him this. She skirted the chair and sat back down. "Some correspondence caught up to me several months ago. Among all the other things I received was a letter from the lawyer I had used in Mexico." She shrugged. "I'm not sure of all the details, but apparently, because of another case he was handling, it had come to my lawyer's attention that the proper procedure wasn't followed in our divorce."

"Cut to the bottom line, Jacey."

"I've already told you the bottom line. Our divorce, along with several others he handled during that time, is not valid. We have to get another one."

Philip let out a long, colorful stream of curses. "Beautiful, just beautiful. And damned convenient timing for you, wouldn't you say? Even with the company in trouble, I'm worth considerably more now than I was the first time you divorced me."

She had expected his accusation, so she wasn't hurt. But she *was* saddened. Why couldn't he seem to give her the benefit of the doubt? "Relax, Philip. I don't want anything from you."

"You expect me to believe you?"

"It might be a nice change."

His eyes narrowed on her. "When I kissed you, you responded like—" He broke off. "Did you think I would sweeten the settlement if you got me hot enough?" His expression was almost a sneer. "You must have thought it was at least worth a shot, because you certainly put some effort into that kiss. Congratulations on a great performance."

She carefully kept all emotion from her face. "Are you through?"

"Hell, no. I've only begun. And there's something you'd better know. You're going to have to do better than that one kiss, Jacey. A hell of a lot better. And here's an idea for you—why don't we start now?"

It took an enormous amount of discipline not to get up and run from the room, from his anger, from the treacherous thought that she would enjoy starting immediately. "Are you through now?"

"No way, sweetheart."

"Then do us both a favor and at least take a break and listen to me."

"Sorry. I'm not interested in doing you a favor."

"Then do it for yourself."

The lines of his mouth turned cruel. "Make it worth my while."

"Dammit, Philip, listen to me!"

She didn't think she had ever raised her voice to him before, but she probably should have done it sooner, because his attention was now riveted on her.

She let out a long breath. "First of all, you know that I have all the money I need. Between my father and yours, I'm well provided for."

"True, but with more money you could buy your own jet. Think about it, Jacey. You wouldn't have to depend on airline schedules."

She sighed and rubbed her forehead. "Look, I'm as upset about this as you are."

Yes, she would be upset, he thought, opening and closing his hand. But was he? Lord, he didn't know. He tried to rein in his ever-increasing tension and think. When he had awakened the next morning after spending that one night with her, he had been alone. It wasn't right that she had simply gotten up and left without waking him. Lying there in the bed where he had taken her virginity, in the bed that still smelled of their lovemaking, he thought about what had occurred.

Shock was his first emotion. His wanting her had been growing with each year, but he'd have liked to think he would never have acted upon that want, except . . . there she had been, in his bedroom, soft and sweet, with a dangerous combination of ripe innocence and unquestioning willingness in her eyes.

Guilt. Lord, the emotion fairly clawed at him. She was still so young, a virgin, plus she was his stepsister. He asked himself over and over again how he could have reached for her as he had and taken her. Then he asked himself how he could have not done it.

Self-reproach. He was filled with it. But despite the blame he heaped on himself, he couldn't find it in himself to regret the night that had just passed. In fact, he was left with a terrible consuming need of her and a determination to make her his.

He knew he was going to have to eventually face their parents, but that prospect didn't bother him half as much as having to face Jacey again. He had no idea what she felt for him. She might hate him for all he knew.

Masking his uncertainties with a cloak of steel-like resolve, and shielding his fears with an over-bearing arrogance, he stormed down to her room. He found her sitting in the window seat, hugging that ridiculous stuffed bear to her. He insisted that she marry him, and she responded to him with a remote wariness. In the end, he got her to agree. She married him, and then he lost her.

He came back to the present and found her watching him, remote and wary as ever. "So what happened? Did the court clerk have one too many margaritas that day?"

"Something like that, I guess. I'm not really sure. Looking back, I should have followed up better. It was a little town, and everything was pretty laid back down there. Everyone I came in contact with smiled constantly. I should have known they were too happy to be worrying about details. At any rate, we need to keep our situation in perspective. It could be worse. One or both of us could have remarried, and then we'd have to deal with the bigamy factor."

"Yes, sir, we are definitely lucky."

His sarcasm scraped jaggedly along her irritated nerves. She clenched her hands together in her lap. "I think we are." She hesitated as she considered another angle. "But then, I'm not involved with anyone. What I mean is, I don't foresee wanting to marry in the next few months, but maybe your situation is different." She waited for him to say something, and when he didn't, she went on. "If that's the case, I'm truly sorry."

"It's not the case," he said quietly.

"Good." She was relieved because there would be no added complications, she told herself. No other reason. "You don't have to worry about a thing. I already have an appointment with my lawyer, and when I see him, I'll have him start the proceedings immediately."

"Then you plan to get a divorce in this country?"

She nodded. "Since there's no reason for us to be in a big rush, I might as well stay and see that it's done right this time."

Keeping his eyes on her, he picked up a pencil and twirled it between his fingers. "Stay?"

"In the state of New York."

"But not here at the house?"

"I'd like to remain here for a couple of more weeks, but if you'd rather I didn't—"

He made an impatient sound. "You can stay as long as you like."

"Thank you."

"Oh, for crying out loud, Jacey, quit being so damned formal."

She looked down at her intertwined fingers. Her knuckles were white. She pulled her hands apart and felt no better. She was crazy to stay there. "I'd like to spend some time with Mother. After that, I'll probably go back to my apartment in the city."

He glanced at the pencil, a small smile playing around his mouth. "You know, Jacey, I find this unexpected turn of events rather interesting."

She had expected his curses. She had even expected the accusations. But she hadn't expected the smile. "Interesting? What do you mean?"

"You're still my wife."

She couldn't read him. Never had been able to. But if she'd ever wished for the power, she wished for it now. "I'm not sure what you're saying."

He wasn't either. Except . . . now that he had forced himself to calm down somewhat, the thought that Jacey was his wife was an oddly exciting one. They were bonded together legally, if in no other way. "Don't you think it's interesting that you and I are married, and in fact have been married for the last ten years." He paused, searching for words, wondering what they would be, and wondering if he really wanted to say them. "Doesn't it make you wonder if we might have lived the last six years differently if we had known?"

She had just spent endless days and weeks in a Bombay hospital room thinking of very little else. She chose her next words carefully. "What is it that you think we might have done differently?"

"Oh, I don't know." His lips quirked, and his eyes glittered as he looked at her. "Maybe you might have made it home for at least one, maybe two Christmases." He paused. "Who knows? You might have even decided to give the idea of marriage a chance."

She almost fell out of the chair. "*Me?* Not *you?*"

He nodded. "Okay, point taken. I was there too." But he'd been so full of hurt, anger, and pride, and so busy trying to prove himself. . . . But despite it all, he knew he had no excuses.

She sighed a soft, almost inaudible sound. "What's the use of wondering, Philip? Those years are gone, and our lives are completely different now from what they were then. Besides, we were never really married, not in the true sense of the word. We never even lived together as man and wife."

"No, you're right. We didn't. We had just that one night."

She smoothed a hand back and forth across her forehead, realizing she was getting a headache. For an instant, fear seized her that this one would be as bad as the last one, but she felt compelled to stay for at least a few more minutes. She considered this conversation too important to walk out on. "All I can say is that I'm genuinely sorry about the mix-up with the divorce. I was just trying to get it as fast as I could."

"Yeah," he said softly, "I know."

Something in the tone of his voice caught her attention and lifted her defenses even higher. "It's been six years, Philip. And not once had you ever given me any indication—" The hurt of that time, the heartbreak. It all came back to her, and she felt as if it were happening once again. She stared down at her hands.

"You're right," he said with a strange rasp to his voice. "I didn't. But then, I could say the same thing for you."

She glanced up at him and saw that his eyes were very dark, and for some reason that she couldn't fathom, her heart began to pound heavily. "What-what are you—"

Abruptly he gave an impatient shake of his head. "Nothing. Nothing at all. As you said, what's the point." He tossed the pencil down. "And, Jacey, this isn't your fault, so quit apologizing. Now that we know, we'll do whatever we have to do to rectify the matter."

Rectify the matter. The phrase sounded like such an impersonal ending to something that had been very personal, she thought. But in truth, the personal part had lasted only hours, and now it was ten years later.

"I have just one question."

She tensed and was at a loss to understand why. Despite the accusations, he had actually been much more reasonable than she had expected. "What is it?"

"You said you received the lawyer's letter several months ago. What took you so long to let me know?"

She had been too sick to let him know, but more than ever she was determined to keep that knowledge from him. "I was having such a good time, I didn't want to interrupt my trip." Her answer invited sarcasm, and she prepared herself for his biting retort. To her surprise, his reply was disconcertingly thoughtful.

"What exactly is it about traveling that you love so much, Jacey? I mean, I enjoy traveling myself, but it seems to me that *constant* traveling would be wearing."

And lonely, she mentally added. Very lonely.

She shrugged. "It's exciting to go to faraway places, to see new things and meet new people." It was true to a point, but she had recently come to the conclusion that the reason she traveled had nothing to do with new places or people.

No. It had to do with running.

• • •

There hadn't been a time in the past few months when she hadn't been able to drop into a deep sleep the minute she shut her eyes, but her conversation with Philip had left her too keyed up to sleep. She still had her headache, but instead of the blinding, gripping pain of several nights before, it was a dull, vague pain, and she resisted reaching for the pain pills.

Willing herself to relax, she lay still, and her mind drifted past the pain to that early morning ten years before when she had awakened beside Philip. Her body had throbbed in a new, embarrassingly satisfied way, a reminder of the hours they had just spent together. Humiliation had washed over her in waves. He would now think the worst of her, and he had every reason to. She had been shameless.

Tears had coursed down her face as she had sneaked from his room and returned to hers. Slipping under the shower, she had scrubbed her young body until her skin had turned red and her tears had stopped flowing. Then, exhausted and wrapped in her oldest, most comfortable bathrobe, she had curled up in her window seat and hugged her teddy bear to her.

She had been painfully aware that she had pushed herself on Philip, but she hadn't been able to stop herself. She had fancied that she understood how terribly hurt he was that Marcus wouldn't listen to his ideas, and she had wanted desperately to comfort him.

And so she went to him.

She hadn't known she was capable of feeling the way he had made her feel. Her mother had told her about sex in a clear, concise way, giving her all the facts, clearing her throat several times as she did. But she had never mentioned one word about passion.

No. In the heat of the night, Jacey learned that for herself.

There was initial discomfort, but it passed, and under Philip's tutelage she discovered passion.

To make matters worse, he burst into her room and, to her horror, demanded that she marry him. She supposed she yearned to be wooed and courted, but there was no sign of love or romance in his demand, and it was plain to her that he felt forced to marry her. His peremptory attitude fed her insecurities and uncertainties.

But in the end she went along with him— because she loved him, and because, deep inside, she harbored the naive hope that one day he would come to love her as much as she did him.

Her expectations proved to be extremely naive. Insisting that they keep everything a secret from their parents, he rushed the wedding, calling a school friend whose father was a judge. As a favor to Philip, the man cut through the red tape. Before she had time to fully think through her decision, she was standing beside Philip, numbly repeating the marriage vows. Then immediately after the short ceremony was over, he turned to her and, with a hard expression, told her he was taking her home so that she could pack.

His bald statement was like throwing cold water in her face. He was asking her to leave the safety and security of what she knew and go into an unknown future with someone who hadn't shown her even one sign of affection since he had taken her virginity, who hadn't even kissed her when they had been pronounced man and wife.

At that moment, what little courage she had

managed to hang on to drained away, and she balked. But she hadn't given up completely, and she came up with a compromise. It had been her hope that he would stay with her at the house, at least until they could get to truly know each other. When she had timidly proposed the idea, he had flatly refused, though, and had left. Two weeks later, after spending endless heart-wrenching hours waiting for him to come see her or at the very least to call, she went off to college.

For a long while she held out hope that he would come to her, apologize, and confess his love. But that never happened. As time passed, her heartbreak didn't so much fade as a protective shell grew around it, and after graduation, she flew to Mexico to get a divorce. Neither Marcus nor her mother ever knew that their children had been married.

Her thoughts drifted back to the present and to the persistent headache she still had. She got up, took one pain pill, then returned to bed. Slowly the memories faded and she eased into a deep sleep.

Philip drummed his fingers on the windowsill in his office early the next afternoon. *Jacey was late.*

The office was a large corner room located on the second floor of a two-story building that sat directly across a narrow drive from the sprawling plant.

He glared down at the drive, as if by sheer force of will he could make her appear there. Dammit, where was she?

The knots in his stomach were tightening, multiplying. Fighting off Bryan and his father was going to be hard; without Jacey's support it would be virtually impossible. And she was coming today to judge him and the decisions he had made for the company.

He supposed he shouldn't take it so personally, but he couldn't help himself. Right or wrong—and he was willing to admit that more than likely there were times when he had been wrong—he had given up a lot for this company.

Ten years ago he had made a stand with both his father and Jacey, an all-or-nothing stand.

He had ended up with nothing.

Raw, wounded, hurting, he left them both. Using the money he inherited from his mother, he started his own company and in a relatively short time made a success of it. After his father's death, the board of directors of KillaneTech gave him, as majority stockholder and Marcus's son, the opportunity to come back home and head the company. The chance to prove that he had been right was irresistible. He sold his company and invested the proceeds in KillaneTech.

And then he proceeded to work harder than he ever had before. To prove to his father that his business theories had been sound and valid. To prove to Jacey that she had been right that night to walk down that hall to his room to comfort him. To prove to her that she should have come to live with him when he had asked her to.

With a curse he crossed to a bookshelf and picked up a gold-framed photograph. It was a picture of Jacey taken at her high school graduation. Her head was back, her golden hair shining in the afternoon sunlight, and she was laughing with a carefree abandon. As always, he was riveted by the utter happiness the camera had captured. Edith had told him that his father had taken the picture. He wished he could have been there to see that look on her face, but he hadn't been able to make it home until a week later. As it turned out, maybe he shouldn't have come home at all.

Frowning, he replaced the photograph. At his desk he stared unseeingly at a stack of papers. Dammit, he shouldn't be so tense about Jacey. He was dead certain of the decisions he had made and of what he had accomplished. He just wished he could be as certain about his motives.

He kneaded the tightened muscles of his neck and reflected back over the last few days. There was no getting around it. No matter what she said, he couldn't help but feel that something was not quite right, something she hadn't told him, something she was hiding. . . .

Just then the door opened to his office, and she walked in, wearing a classically designed sand-colored sweater and skirt and matching flats. Her hair was swept back from her face and held at the nape of her neck with a gold clip. She looked annoyingly composed and serene. "You're late."

The irritation in his voice sent her brows arching. "I don't remember specifying an exact time."

"No, I suppose you didn't," he muttered, upset with his impatience for her to arrive. "And of course I don't have anything better to do than to wait for you, so it's all right."

Last night when they had parted, he had seemed almost mellow, she reflected wryly, but his mood was definitely different today. Instead of a porcupine, she was dealing with a cobra. Giving herself a chance to become accustomed to his new mood, she gazed around the office, taking in the new furnishings and decorations made of dark wood, soft leather, and shining brass. It looked comfortable, solid, and very masculine. "There've been some changes. Is this the furniture you had in your other company?"

His expression remained dark, but he nodded. "Some of it. Some of it I bought when I took over."

"I like it." She slowly walked around the room, unwilling just yet to give him her entire attention. He was always a shock to her system, but in this mood he could cause a full-out electrocution. At the bookshelf, the gold-framed photograph of herself caught her attention. Astonished, she picked it up.

"I had forgotten this," she murmured.

He hadn't intended to go to her side, but suddenly he was there, inhaling the perfumed scent of her skin and hair. "You looked as if you were really happy."

"I was." Only one cloud had marred the sunshine of that day for her, she remembered. Philip hadn't been able to attend the ceremony. "Where on earth did you get this?"

"Edith gave it to me." He reached out and touched the glass-covered picture, tracing the outlines of her smile.

His finger was long, his nail clean and short. The pad of his finger would be . . . Disconcertingly, her lips tingled, as if he were really touching her. Disturbed more than she was willing to admit, she replaced the picture and turned to the one next to it, one of her mother and Marcus. "She must have given you this one too."

"I asked for both."

She looked up at him with surprise. "You did?"

He shrugged, somewhat uncomfortable at the revelation he had just made. His asking for the pictures might be interpreted as needfulness of some kind. "Why not? Most people have pictures of their family in their offices."

"Yes, but—"

"He was my father, Jacey. Even if I couldn't get along with him, I loved him."

No one could understand that statement as she could, she thought ruefully, but it didn't explain why he had her picture.

"I should have made a greater effort to get along with him."

An old, deeply buried, entirely instinctive urge to comfort him surfaced. "We all have things we regret, Philip."

He looked at her. "Maybe, but there are a great many things I regret."

That puzzled her. It seemed to her he had lived just as he had wanted. "What things?"

He touched her face, lightly brushing his finger along her cheek. Voltage zapped through her. She went still. His next words almost stopped her heartbeat.

"What's changed in you, Jacey? What took you from that happy, laughing girl in the picture to the person you are today?"

"What's wrong with the way I am?" she asked guardedly.

"Not a thing, if you're the type who likes a beautiful, inaccessible glacier."

"I wasn't aware that I gave that impression."

"Yes, Jacey, you were."

Yes, she was. She felt safe behind her shield of cool remoteness. She moved her head, pulling away from his hand.

An expression flashed across his face, too quickly for her to decide whether or not it had been pain.

"Was it me?" he asked softly. "Did I do it?"

"No—" The word stuck in her throat. She swallowed and tried again. "Of course not."

"Then who?" What?"

"I'm not sure what you're trying to get at."

He wasn't either, except he felt driven to push forward. "Have there been many other men?"

She stiffened.

"I'm sure every man you meet is challenged by you." His voice was hoarse with inner tension. "How many have there been?"

He wouldn't believe her if she told him. She barely believed it herself. But there had been no one before or since him. "Stop it," she whispered.

"I'm interested. Tell me. How many? Ten? Fifty? A hundred?"

"A hundred," she said, her teeth clenched.

"Only a hundred, Jacey? Come on, I have reason to know just exactly how hotblooded you are."

"It might have been a thousand, but I'm not going to tell you, because it's none of your damned business."

"Some people might differ with you. After all"—he touched her again, his fingers sliding down the side of her neck—"I'm your husband."

She jerked away from him. "On paper only, and because of a mistake."

Without warning his tone went flat, and his hand dropped to his side. "*Mistake.* That one word sums up everything about us, doesn't it?"

She immediately regretted the use of the word. "No, I didn't mean—"

He abruptly wheeled for the door. "Are you ready for a tour of the plant?"

His quick mood swings had her thoughts whirling, but without a word, she followed him.

She saw the changes immediately. Work conditions had been improved considerably. Added windows and updated fixtures provided more light, and the new machines were not only more efficient, they had been arranged to maximize space and minimize noise. She was impressed, but for the moment chose to keep her own council.

"Jacey, is that you?"

She turned toward the voice of a man she recognized, Harold Willis, a longtime employee of the company.

"Mr. Willis, how nice to see you."

He took her hand and pumped it enthusiastically. "The same here, young lady. The same here."

She smiled. "Let's see. You had a daughter, didn't you? How is she? If I remember correctly, she must be about ready to graduate from high school."

He beamed with pride. "You remember right, and she's won herself a scholarship to college." His eyes slid to Philip. "One of KillaneTech's new scholarships for the kids of its employees."

She glanced at Philip. "Really? What a wonderful idea. And, Mr. Willis, congratulations. Be sure to tell your daughter I said good luck."

"I'll do that."

As they continued, Philip stayed at her side, guiding her, explaining and pointing out details. He almost resented it when she stopped to speak to people. And he *did* resent the genuine warmth and interest she showed them. A thought almost stopped him in his tracks. He was jealous, pure and simple.

Sometime later Jacey cast a discreet look at her watch and was surprised to find they had been in the plant for only a little over an hour. She had seen and learned a great deal that confirmed beliefs she already held. If she were honest with herself, she would admit that she hadn't needed a tour to know that Philip had done a superb job. When she cut through the tangle of her emotions and feelings, she still had the faith in him that she had had ten years earlier, at least where the company was concerned. Insisting on coming today had been merely an effort to assert herself, but now she could feel weariness creeping in, and she knew she should leave soon.

She spied another familiar figure up ahead, an older woman with frosted hair and a round, friendly face. "Mrs. DeAngelo, how are you?"

"Why, Jacey, how nice to see you. It's been too long. My, you're still as pretty as a picture."

She was used to compliments, but not when they were given under Philip's eagle-eyed gaze. "Thank you," she said, and hurried on to another subject. "How's that son of yours? His name is Bill, isn't it?"

Apparently it was the wrong subject. Mrs. DeAngelo's expression changed, tightened. "*Bill's* fine, but that girl he married isn't worth two cents. Her idea of dinner is a jar of peanut butter and a loaf of bread. Can you imagine?"

Since she wasn't an inspired cook herself, she felt compelled to go to the girl's defense. "Maybe she'll learn to cook as time goes by."

"They've been married three years. How much time does she need, I ask you? What am I going to do when grandchildren come along? Watch them starve?"

"Have you thought about giving her cooking lessons for Christmas?"

"No, but that's not a bad idea."

Jacey felt Philip's hand on her elbow, gently urging her to move on.

"Sorry, Mrs. DeAngelo," Philip said, "but Jacey doesn't have much time, and I want her to see everything."

The older woman nodded approvingly. "You take her on, then. Jacey, Philip is doing a great job. We are all one hundred percent behind him."

"Thank you, Mrs. DeAngelo." With his hand at Jacey's back, he dropped his voice so that only she could hear him. "Cooking lessons?"

"Well, I felt sorry for the poor girl. Mrs. DeAngelo is nice, but I imagine she makes an intimidating mother-in-law."

"It's not your problem," he said tersely. "Besides, if you stop to talk to everyone, we'll never get through."

"Sorry. I didn't mean to hold us up, but I didn't realize I would still know so many people, or that they would remember me."

"You did spend a fair amount of your summers here, doing odd jobs, running errands for Dad, that sort of thing."

"I'd forgotten." She glanced at her watch again. "How much more is there to see?"

"A great deal. We aren't even close to being through with the tour."

It had been months since she had done anything half as strenuous, and she was extremely pleased that she had been able to do this much. But the constant walking and standing was taking its toll, and she was beginning to feel a little shaky. She slowed her steps until she came to a stop. "I think I've seen enough."

He frowned, puzzled. "We've barely begun."

"I don't need to see any more. It's obvious—"

The full impact of what she was saying hit him. "No, Jacey. You wanted to see what I've done, and you're going to see it. Before you leave here and go home to make up your mind, you're going to have all the facts."

"I've seen enough."

His forehead pleated in bewilderment. "What are you talking about? We've hardly scratched the surface. You need to see everything. I don't want you to have any excuses not to make the right decision."

Her eyes flashed with rare temper. "The right decision being *your* way?"

"Interpret it however you wish, but you're going to get the full tour."

His expression was hard with determination, his hand against her back firm. With a small push he started her forward again, toward a staircase. "Let's take a quick detour upstairs. I've done some things up there I want you to see."

They were still on the second level an hour and a half later, when Jacey realized she couldn't go much farther. Her legs had turned to rubber, and her head was beginning to hurt. She stopped as they neared an elevator. "How much more is there to see?" she asked, infusing her voice with a strength she didn't feel.

"We've got the new addition yet, plus—"

She shook her head, her features firmly set. "Sorry, but I'll have to see it some other time. I need to go home."

She was trying to leave again, and he had so much more he wanted her to see, so much more he was proud of. He wanted to see admiration in her eyes for all he had done, he wanted to hear compliments on her soft lips. "What do you mean *need*? What's wrong? What are you up to, Jacey?"

"I just need to go home, that's all, and I've seen enough." She punched the elevator button. "By the way, for what it's worth, you've done a terrific job."

She had given him a compliment. Why didn't he feel better? "Does that mean that you'll vote your stock with me?"

She was minutes away from losing her ability to carry on an intelligent conversation. "That's what it means, but we'll have to talk about the details later."

He should be shouting for joy, but there was something wrong. . . .

The elevator doors opened, and gratefully, she darted in. Unfortunately, Philip followed her.

As soon as the doors closed, he backed her against the wall and pinned her with a hand on either side of her head. "No way, Jacey. You're not leaving until I understand what's going on with you. This company might provide part of your income, but it's far more than that to me. I've poured a fair share of my blood into it, and I don't intend to let Bryan or his father or anyone else come in and take it over."

He was too close, she thought, his body heat too encompassing. She couldn't fight against the weakness of both her body *and* her emotions. She shut her eyes just as the elevator stopped its descent. She heard him punch a button and the doors stayed closed. Lord, she was trapped with him.

"Look, Philip, I plan to do everything in my power to help you, I promise. What more can I say?"

Frustration pounded in his brain and in his blood. "You can say something I can believe."

She almost groaned aloud, because she didn't believe what he was asking was possible. "Do such words even exist? Do they, Philip?"

He hit the wall by her head with the flat of his hand. "Dammit, I don't understand you. I'm trying to save my company and you . . . you— What in the hell are you doing, Jacey? Do you even know?"

Strangely enough, she sympathized with him and understood what he was going through. "You're going to have to trust me, Philip," she said quietly. "It's really all you can do."

Was it really all he could do? he wondered, gazing down at her, frustrated and ill tempered. She looked like a statue of some ancient mythic goddess, pale, still, and cool as alabaster. And too lovely to be real. But dammit, she was. She was his wife. And the idea was eating at him.

"Jacey." His tone wasn't questioning. He had simply said her name, his voice deep and dark.

She didn't move, didn't respond; his nerves drew even more taut until he wasn't sure how he was going to deal with the pain. He clamped his hand along her jawline. "Dammit, Jacey. Look at me."

She didn't want to. She was afraid of what she might see. Anger, hatred . . . heat. She wouldn't be able to handle any of those from him.

He lowered himself against her, slowly increasing the pressure until she could feel every hard muscle and enticing bulge of his lean, powerful body. She had always had a weakness where he was concerned, and now, because of her physically depleted condition, she seemed to be more vulnerable to him than ever, in grave danger of losing her pride, her dignity, and her self-respect. She tried to push him away, but her attempt was woefully feeble.

Suddenly his mouth was on hers, and she was hit by the simultaneous heat and shock of his kiss. And at that moment she lost even a prayer of defending herself. Her response came easily, quickly. Her lips automatically parted, as if all he had to do was touch his mouth to hers and she would willingly open to him. Her body forgot that it was recovering from a serious illness, and for the first time in months she came alive. Passion gave her new strength, and she wound her arms around his neck and arched against him. When he deepened his kiss, she clung tighter.

He was in one of the company's elevators, Philip thought distantly, the same company where countless people worked, many of them not too far from where he was now. And all he could think of was Jacey and how much he wanted her. He was mad—mad for her.

He slipped his hand beneath her sweater and encountered a lacy bra. For a moment he allowed himself the luxury of tracing the openwork design and imagining how her skin must look through the figured fabric. The lace was delicate and no doubt fragile, but it didn't occur to him to take care as he skimmed his hand beneath the bra to one firm breast.

A small cry escaped from her mouth to his, a cry of delight. Beneath his touch she was heated liquid, ebbing and flowing in rhythm to his kisses and touches. Time and place were lost to her. Sensation after sensation swamped her.

Her nipple pearled against his palm. Urgency pounded through him. He wanted to draw the taut bud into his mouth and taste her again. And that was only the beginning of what he wanted. He was hungry for her, desperate for her, burning up inside for her. He ground his pelvis against hers.

She barely heard the elevator bell. His tongue was doing a primal dance with hers, entwining, retreating, entwining. His hand was kneading her breast. . . .

He heard the bell and knew it meant that someone wanted the elevator. Another few seconds and he would have pulled her down to the floor with him. He still might. With a curse he jerked away. "Jacey, open your eyes and look at me." His voice was little more than a grinding sound.

The heat still held her in its grip, and his order confused her.

"Jacey, we've got to get out of here."

Her lashes fluttered, then lifted, and she looked up at him. The intensity of his gaze seared her to her bones. *What had she done?*

He studied her critically, trying to fight against his need of her. He failed. A delicate blush stained her cheeks, her lips were reddened and already puffed and swollen from his kisses, and parts of her silky hair had slipped free of its gold clip. She looked beautiful and thoroughly kissed.

And delicious.

He lowered his head, intent on finishing what he had started, but the bell sounded again, and he was assailed by the unshakable urge to fire the person responsible.

With a shaking hand he tugged her sweater down until he was satisfied that it was straight, then he jabbed the Open button. The doors swished open and Jacey bolted for the exit of the plant.

He walked out of the elevator after her, but soon slowed his steps until he came to a stop. Slipping his hands into his trouser pockets, he stared after her, a grim expression on his face.

One way or the other, he thought, Jacey was going to be the ruination of him.

Six

It was already dark outside when Philip arrived home. He went straight to his study. Once there, he dropped into the chair behind his desk just as he had done a thousand times before. But unlike all those other times, he simply sat, gazing blindly into the darkness.

A few minutes later, when Barton quietly knocked on the door and entered, he hadn't even turned on the desk light or opened his briefcase.

"Good evening, Mr. Killane." When Philip didn't answer, Barton proceeded to the desk and switched on the lamp.

Philip blinked at the sudden light.

"The cook was wondering about your plans, sir. Will you be having dinner in this evening?"

"No." He didn't want to have to sit at the table with Jacey and Edith, trying to make polite conversation when all the while he was remembering how close he had come to making love to Jacey in the elevator. He swiped a hand over his face, wishing he could erase the memory as easily. "I mean, I won't be having dinner in the dining room, but I would like a tray in here later. I'll call when I'm ready."

Barton nodded. "Very good."

If he told Barton he had invited twelve alligators to dinner, the man would still say very good, Philip thought vaguely. "Is everyone else eating in to-night?" He grimaced at his lack of courage. Why couldn't he ask straight out if Jacey was going to be home tonight? It was what he wanted to know.

"No, sir. Mrs. Killane is going out for the evening, and Miss Killane said if she got hungry, she'd call for a tray later."

"*If* she got hungry? Where is she now?"

"In her room, sir. Will that be all?"

"Yes, thank you, Barton."

Philip closed his eyes and leaned his head back against the chair. There must be a hundred things he should be doing right at this moment, but he couldn't seem to think of one. Everything had been so clear to him before Jacey had come home, he reflected tiredly. Saving the company had been his top priority, and it still was. But somehow Jacey was requiring more and more of his time, both mentally and physically. She kept crowding into his mind, muddying issues and twisting feelings, until he wasn't sure what was or wasn't important. And his body stayed in a heightened state of demand and need, confusing him, annoy-ing the hell out of him, causing him pain.

She had said she was going to vote the stock his way, that she was going to help him. And then she hadn't been able to get away from him fast enough.

He didn't understand her actions. He most def-initely didn't like them. But he at least knew she hadn't left the plant because of what happened between them in the elevator. She was already in the process of leaving when he had kissed her. And for those few minutes, she had turned sweet, hot, pliant. . . .

He rubbed his eyes. Why did he still want her after all these years? Why couldn't he take her words at face value? And why the hell couldn't he seem to trust her?

He glanced at the study door. Maybe if he heard her say again that she would vote her stock with him, it would help him. Maybe if he could see her . . .

Outside Jacey's door Philip lifted his hand and knocked. When after a minute she didn't appear, he knocked once more. But again there was no answer.

He frowned. He supposed she might have left the room and gone downstairs to the kitchen or sitting room while he was still in his study.

He turned the knob and walked in. Light from the adjoining bathroom sliced across the floor in the otherwise dark room and helped him make out Jacey. She was in her bed, sound asleep.

He crossed to the bedside table, picked up the clock, and read its luminescent numbers. Seven-thirty, far too early for anyone to be asleep for the night. He replaced the clock and clicked on the lamp. "Jacey?"

She didn't move. He stared down at her, knowing he should leave, but staying anyway.

She hadn't pulled the covers over her, so he could see that she was wearing a nightgown, a slim column of blue satin with tiny straps. The gown's hem grazed her ankles, and her hair was a sleek swirl over her shoulders. It was as if she hadn't moved since she lay down. She must have been really tired. But why?

Dammit, a better question would be what was he doing in her room like this, watching her sleep. He needed to get the hell out of there.

He sat down on the bed beside her. "Jacey, wake up."

Her breasts moved slightly as she inhaled and exhaled, but otherwise, she didn't stir.

His frown intensified. Surely it wasn't natural for her to be in such a deep sleep at this early hour of the evening. Alarm darted through him. He put his hand on her shoulder and shook. "Jacey, wake up. It's Philip."

She moaned and shifted an arm, but she didn't open her eyes.

He slid his hand from her shoulder down to her arm, intending to shake her again. Then he caught sight of the discolored skin on the inside of her elbow. The normally white skin there was marred by a large purplish-yellow bruise.

He looked closer and his heart began to thud.

Needle marks.

"Dammit, Jacey, wake up!" He leaned over her, gripped both her shoulders, and shook hard.

Jacey fought her way up through the heavy layers of sleep and opened her eyes to see Philip's face above her, his expression dark. She came instantly awake. Her first thought was to wonder what she had done. Her second was to wonder what was he doing in her room, sitting on her bed.

"Sweet heaven, Jacey, you *are* on drugs. How could you be so damned stupid? How could you *do* such a thing to yourself?"

"What?" She understood what he was saying, she just wasn't sure why he was saying it. And there was something else, she realized. He was more than angry. He was *troubled*.

"Can you sit up?"

"Yes, but—"

Without waiting for her to complete her answer, he slipped his hands beneath her shoulders, shifted the pillows behind her into a mound against the headboard, then lifted her until she was in a half-sitting position.

"Now, tell me about it," he said, fixing her with a determined gaze. "I want to know everything. What are you on? How long? And where is it?"

She squirmed, uncomfortable beneath his intense scrutiny. The last time she had seen him, he had been kissing her and had held her bare breast in his hand. Now he was looking at her with an accusatory stare. Fleetingly, she wished she were wearing more than a mere nightgown. Given her choice of attire for this moment, she would choose armor. She rubbed her eyes, trying to shake off the lingering drowsiness of her sleep. "Haven't we had this conversation before?"

"Only part of it." The lines of his mouth were grim. "I asked you if you were on drugs, and you said no, and I let it go. This time I'm not about to let it go."

He might be upset, but he was still Philip, she thought. And he was sitting very close to her. That meant her body was responding whether she wanted it to or not. She crossed her arms beneath her breasts. "If I remember correctly, this is the third time you've accused me of being on drugs in spite of the fact that I've told you I'm not. Tell me, Philip. What exactly is it about me that makes you think I'm lying? Are there drug dealers lining up downstairs? Have you found a cache of drugs? What *is* it?"

He grabbed her arm and held it straight out. "This." His eyes flashed with fiery emotion. "Those needlemarks mean you're into the hard stuff, Jacey. Start at the beginning and tell me everything, including where you keep the drugs and the needles. The drugs are getting flushed down the toilet. I don't know what the hell I'll do with the needles, but count on it, I'll do something. Then I'm going to get you help. You're going to get straight, because I'm not going to leave you alone until you're free of the stuff. And *then*, dammit, you're going to stay straight if I have to keep you under lock and key for the rest of your life."

She was almost speechless. Almost. "Let's just get this one little thing cleared up between us before we go any further. You are not, I repeat *not*, locking me anywhere. Now that I've said that, tell me something. Why are you so damned quick to think the worst of me? You didn't believe me today when I told you I would vote my stock your way, and now you think I'm a junkie. Do I have shifty eyes? A character flaw I don't know about? *Not to be believed* written across my forehead? Why, Philip?"

He held up her arm again. "Tell me you're not on drugs."

She looked him straight in the eyes. "I'm not."

He flung her arm away with a groan. "How did you let yourself get in such a mess? Was it a man? Did a man get you hooked?" He raked his hands through his hair, digging his fingers into his scalp. "Lord, right after we were married I should have come back here, packed up your things myself, and insisted you come with me."

Her mouth dropped open. "Excuse me? What did you just say?"

"You heard me. If I had done that, this would never have happened." He jerked upright from the bed and headed for the chest of drawers. "Where's the stuff, Jacey?" He opened a drawer and pawed through her things.

Briefly she closed her eyes and squeezed the bridge of her nose with her thumb and forefinger. "Philip, there are no drugs."

He didn't even pause in his search, going from one drawer to the next.

"Listen to me, Philip. I had a blood test yesterday when I went into the city to have lunch with Bryan. The nurse had trouble finding a vein, and she must have poked me at least a half-dozen times before she found one. It left a bruise."

He slammed the last drawer in the chest shut and strode to the dresser. "You expect me to believe that?"

She sighed. "No, I suppose I don't." She pushed herself off the bed, walked to the closet, and retrieved the satin robe that went with the gown. The sight of his big hands delving through her delicate lingerie gave her a shivery feeling that she hoped wearing the robe would help. "By the way, you *will* straighten anything you mess up."

He hit the top of the dresser with a closed fist, so hard the mirror shook. "Dammit, Jacey, how can I believe you? You've changed. Something's different about you. If it's not drugs, then you tell me what it is."

"I'm all grown up now, Philip. That's the difference, the *only* difference."

"No, there's something else. I can't put my finger on it, but there's something. . . ."

She drew a deep breath. "For the last time, I am not on drugs. I had a blood test, that's all."

"For what?"

"What?"

"Why did you go to the doctor and have a blood test?"

For some reason, she hadn't expected him to ask that question. Maybe it was because she was still reeling from the idea that he thought he should have made her go with him after they were married. "I've been feeling tired lately—you know that—and—"

"You said it was jet lag."

He had actually stopped his search and was listening to her. Cautiously Jacey regarded it as a sign of victory. Just as cautiously she chose her next words. "I thought that it was. I still do. It's just that I didn't think it would hurt to get myself checked out."

He took a step toward her. "And?"

"And what?" she asked blankly.

"And what were the results?"

"Oh. The results from the test aren't back yet, but the doctor examined me and couldn't find anything wrong. He was confident that the test results would show the same." It was almost the truth.

He closed the distance between them and lifted her arm. He pushed the sleeve of the robe back until he could examine the bruise. He studied the area for a long minute, then lightly stroked his fingers across it. "Why can't I believe you?"

Because somehow, she thought, he sensed it was *almost* the truth, not the entire truth. "More than likely, it's because you don't like me very much and you never have."

"That's not true."

"Oh, no? It sounds to me as if you still resent the fact that I didn't come with you after we were married."

His smile caught her unaware and chilled her to the bone.

"Is it so strange for a groom to expect his bride to come live with him?"

She simply wasn't up to a discussion of their past tonight, she thought, jerking her arm away. "I'm not a junkie, Philip. Believe me. Accept it. And get out of my room."

His smile never wavered. "No." He walked around her and picked up her purse off the dresser.

Outraged at the invasion of her privacy, she gasped and reached for the purse. "Don't you *dare* go through my purse!"

He jerked it out of her reach. She lunged for it and managed to knock it out of his hand. It fell to the floor, the catch snapped open, and everything in it spilled out.

Horrified, she stared down at the contents. Lying among her handkerchief, her compact, her coin purse, her lipstick, and her checkbook was her bottle of pain pills.

She bent to reach for it, but he was there first, scooping it up. When she straightened, he was reading the label.

"I thought you said you weren't on drugs."

"I—I'm not."

"This is one of the most powerful painkillers a doctor can prescribe, Jacey, and the bottle is nearly empty."

He spoke very quietly, yet his voice vibrated with a terrible fury. She decided she would rather have him shout at her. "It's half full."

"Okay, so it's half full. Have you or have you not taken the other half?"

She was going to have to tell him, she thought reluctantly. She had tried hard to keep her secret, but now it seemed she had no alternative. She waved her hand toward a chair. "Sit down, Philip, and I'll tell you everything."

"I think I'd rather stand." His voice was still quiet, but his tone had turned wooden, as if he were dreading what he was about to hear.

She gave him a brief, sad smile. "It's not going to be as bad as you expect."

"I'd still rather stand."

She nodded. "All right. *I'll* sit." She perched on the end of the bed, linked her hands together, and stared down at them, gathering her thoughts.

"Start with the pills."

Why not? she thought wearily. It was as good a place as any to start. "You're right. They're very strong pain pills, but I'm not hooked on them. That's the only bottle I was ever given, and they were prescribed for headaches."

"You told me you didn't get headaches often."

She moved her hand, a gesture that meant nothing. "I'm much better."

His eyes narrowed. "What do you mean better? Better than what exactly?"

Lord, she'd give anything if she didn't have to tell him. She drew a deep breath. "I've been very sick, Philip. I picked up a virus while I was in India."

His voice went even quieter and, in the process, somehow became even more ominous. "Does this virus have a name?"

"Yes, but even if I told you, you wouldn't know it. It's an extremely rare and exotic type of virus that had the doctors fooled for quite a while, and it can be picked up only over there."

"Define very sick."

She looked away. "I almost died."

There was silence. The silence stretched, expanding and lengthening, filling the room.

Then there was an explosion as Philip let loose with a long, colorful stream of curses. When he was finished, he looked at her, shocked and appalled. "Why in the hell didn't you tell me before now?"

She shrugged, but she felt anything but nonchalant. "There was no need. The worst is past, and I'm on the mend."

"I assume this happened in Bombay?"

She nodded.

"And you were in the hospital over there?"

"Yes."

"Jacey, why in the hell didn't you have them notify me? Or your mother?"

That was a hard question for her to answer. She had been asked many times if there was someone they could contact for her, but she had always said no. "I guess the truth is I felt too estranged from both of you to want you there to watch me die."

He cursed again. "Dammit, Jacey. I could have helped. I could have arranged to have you flown home to a hospital here."

"I wouldn't have made it here alive."

All the color drained from his face. "Then I could have flown specialists to you."

"The doctors in Bombay were better equipped to find out what was wrong since the virus originated there. There was nothing you could have done, Philip. I was either going to die or get better."

His voice dropped to a whisper. "But at least if you had died, you wouldn't have been alone."

"What difference would that have made? I've lived all my adult life alone."

Strangely affected by that idea, he snapped back at her. "Where the hell were your friends?"

He hadn't understood what she meant, she thought sadly. That even when she was with her friends she had felt alone. To counteract that feeling, she had kept moving, circling the globe. "I had been traveling with a group, but when I decided I wanted to go to India, no one else did, so I went off on my own."

She expected him to curse again, but he didn't. He just gazed at her for a long moment. "Are you all right?"

"I'm fine. Really, I am. And I'm getting better all the time."

"Then why were you asleep at seven in the evening?"

She lifted a hand, then let it fall again. "It was the tour today. I'm afraid all that walking got the best of me. The first hour I did pretty well, but the second . . . It was hard."

All at once he understood many of the things that had confused him in the afternoon. "And I insisted you continue."

"You didn't know."

His eyes were so dark, they obscured all expression. "No. Thanks to you, I didn't have a clue. And then I compounded the problem by pushing you against the wall of an elevator and nearly making love to you." He cursed again.

She had no idea how he viewed what had happened between them, but as long as she was being honest, she decided she might as well go all the way. "Yes, you did, but that's where your blame ends. I responded to you."

"But it made you feel worse, didn't it? It must have."

Actually, for those few minutes, she had forgotten all about being tired. "No."

A muscle moved in his jaw. He didn't believe her. "What about the headaches?"

"I had a severe one that first night I was home, and then another one last night that wasn't as bad. They're coming less and less frequently now."

"What brings them on?"

"Stress and fatigue mainly. But I didn't get one today. As I said, I'm really much better."

Stress and fatigue.

She had nearly died.

Alone.

Because she didn't want Edith or him with her.

He looked down at the pill bottle in his hand, trying to imagine how bad her pain must have been for her to require medicine that strong. His imagination came up with something that was damned hard for him to bear.

Slowly he bent, picked up her purse and its contents, and replaced the purse on the dresser. "I'm sorry I woke you up. I'll leave so you can get some rest, but I'm going to have a tray brought up to you. You need to eat."

His voice carried no emotion, and he was moving like someone twice his age. Or someone who carried a tremendous burden. She eyed him curiously. "Why did you come in and wake me? What did you want?"

"It was nothing important. Just something about the company." With his hand on the doorknob, he looked back over his shoulder at her. "It can wait until the morning."

"Please don't go just yet. There's something I want you to know."

"What is it?"

"If I had died in India, you would have received

my shares of KillaneTech stock. It's in my will." He didn't move or say a word, and she continued. "I thought it was only right. After all, the stock belonged to your father."

He walked out of her room and down the hall. Closing the door of his bedroom behind him, he leaned back against it. A tear escaped from his eye and rolled down his cheek. Then another and another. He slid to the floor. With his back against the door, he wrapped his arms around his up-raised knees and let his head fall forward.

When he was nine years old, he had cried at his mother's funeral. It was the last time he had ever cried.

He had felt like crying when Jacey had refused to come with him after their wedding, but he hadn't. He hadn't.

Now, though, the idea of Jacey dying made him want to cry more than anything he had ever known. And she would rather have died alone in a foreign country than have him know she was close to death. He swiped a hand across his damp face. It was a good thing he never cried.

Seven

The next morning Jacey awoke feeling rested and refreshed, at least physically. Mentally, she remained troubled that she had told Philip about her illness. After trying so hard to guard her secret, she felt as if she had given up a part of herself. And she wasn't used to sharing parts of herself.

But strangely enough, taking everything into account, she also felt a certain relief. In retrospect, she could see that trying to hide what had happened to her from Philip had taken a great deal of her energy.

She dressed in jeans and a black and gold sweater and was brushing her hair when she heard the excited bark of a dog. She crossed to the window that overlooked the back lawn. Below her, Philip was throwing a Frisbee to a deliriously happy Douglas.

Captured by the scene of the usually serious Philip playing with his dog, she continued to watch. It was Saturday, and like her, Philip had dressed casually. He was wearing a faded purple sweatshirt, a pair of broken-in tennis shoes, and soft-looking jeans that stretched over the muscles of his long legs as if they'd been especially molded to him. Occasionally he would smile at one of Douglas's antics. He looked fit, relaxed, and maddeningly compelling. But then, he always looked compelling to her, no matter what he wore.

She was wary of seeing him. He hadn't been happy with her last night for keeping her illness a secret. And she was mystified as to why he thought she should have had him notified. She had never been able to view him as her brother, and she had never had the opportunity to view him as a husband. He wasn't even a friend. He was nothing to her. She chewed on her bottom lip, watching him. *Nothing,* she mentally reiterated.

But regardless, there was something she did need to ask him. She tossed the brush onto the bed and went downstairs.

Philip saw her walking across the lawn toward him, her blond hair lying in shining waves around her face and shoulders. He had been waiting to see her, but contradictorily, he wasn't sure he was ready. Seeing her now, he was swamped by emotions that he could neither define or suppress. "I didn't expect you to be up this early."

She glanced at her watch. "It's eight-thirty. That's not early."

"For someone who was as sick as you were, it is."

Please don't let him start hovering over me. The last thing she wanted was for him to see her as a medical problem. Of course that left the question open as to what she *did* want of him. Nothing, she reminded herself. Nothing. "You're right, Philip. *Were.* Past tense."

He made a noncommittal sound, and with a flick of his wrist sent the Frisbee sailing. Douglas took off across the lawn after it, his tongue hanging out, all his energies focused on catching the saucer-shaped disk. At the exact moment the Frisbee started its downward arc, he launched himself upward and snatched it from the air.

She couldn't help but laugh. "Douglas looks like a flying carpet when he jumps up like that, but he's good. I would never have suspected he could move that fast."

"He loves to play," he said, deciding to take her lead and keep the conversation light. "He'll chase anything. A stick, a ball, whatever. But Frisbees are his favorite. I think he regards catching them as a personal challenge." Douglas came bounding up, bearing his prize. Philip bent, took the disk from the dog's mouth, and gave him a scratch behind the ear. "Good boy."

"Is this a Saturday-morning ritual?"

He nodded. "As often as I can manage. In the summertime when it stays light longer I can play with him in the evenings after work." He glanced behind her toward the terrace. "There's Barton with my breakfast. Why don't you join me?"

His invitation caught her by surprise, and she eyed him cautiously, looking for some hidden motive. It was a habit with her, but she also knew it was a habit she needed to break. "Sounds good."

He gestured at Douglas with the Frisbee. "Last one, old man." Douglas barked with excitement. Philip sent the Frisbee flying, and Douglas took off running, his shaggy hair streaming behind him.

Philip put his hand on the small of her back. "Let's go up to the terrace, and you can tell Barton what you'd like."

"All right," she murmured, very much aware of the feel of his hand on her back. It penetrated the thickness of her sweater to her skin, where it spread warmth. Maybe she should have had the doctors in India call Philip to come after all, she thought with dark humor. With a mere touch he could have burned the virus right out of her.

When they reached the terrace, Barton was waiting for them. "Good morning, Miss Killane. Would you like me to set another place?"

She nodded. "Yes, thank you, and I'd also like coffee and a croissant."

Philip shook his head disapprovingly. "That's not much of a breakfast. Barton, bring her a plate of bacon and eggs, along with a bowl of fruit. Oh, and a large glass of fresh orange juice."

Impassively Barton received the order and left.

"Have you ever had the urge to tell him that a family of alligators will be joining you for dinner?" Philip asked her, pulling out a chair and waiting for her to sit down.

Jacey almost fell into the chair. There was actually a twinkle in Philip's eye. "Uh, no, I never have. Have you?"

He nodded, taking a chair across from her. "No, but I've thought about it more than once."

"He's quite wonderful," Jacey said. "You're lucky to have him."

"I know I am. He had several offers when Dad died, but fortunately for us he chose to stay."

Douglas came loping up, dropped the Frisbee, and collapsed in an exhausted heap by Philip's side.

"It wasn't necessary for you to order me such a big breakfast, Philip."

"Yes, it was. A cup of coffee and a croissant aren't going to help you get well." He spared Douglas a glance and a scratch, then fixed her with a penetrating gaze. "So how are you feeling this morning?"

"Fine."

She looked much more than fine, he thought. She looked beautiful. The sweater and jeans fit her loosely, yet managed to display the womanly curves of her body in a ladylike way that made him feel like anything but a gentleman. Her skin was freshly scrubbed and glowed with a hint of natural color in her cheeks. His blood stirred. "Did you eat what I had sent up last night?"

"Most of it." She grimaced. "The portions were huge."

He decided not to tell her that he had fixed the tray himself, or that he had slipped into her room at midnight to assure himself that she had been able to go back to sleep. Or that he had stood there watching her sleep for a long time . . .

"I hope you don't have anything planned today."

She looked at him curiously. "I don't. Why?"

"Because you should rest."

She sighed. "Philip, please don't treat me as if I were an invalid. I'm not."

"You *were*."

"But I'm much better, and I don't want to have to keep telling you. I'm a grown woman. I have enough sense to know when I should rest and when and how much I should eat."

He couldn't help himself; he had to say it. "But not enough sense to know that your mother and I would want to know if you were ill."

Her teeth came together with a snap. "I don't want to talk about it. For better or for worse I made my decision, and now it's done, it's over."

He rubbed his forehead. It had taken duress to get her to admit that she had been sick, and it was still a touchy subject with her. He knew he had to proceed carefully, but he wanted to make sure that she never kept anything of that nature from him again. If she was ever that ill again, he would get her well even if all he had to help him was his sheer will.

"Okay," he said resignedly. "I'd love to argue with you about that particular decision, because I definitely think you could not have made a worse one, but you're right. What's done is done. What's important now is that you take care of yourself."

"Philip—"

Barton reappeared with another place setting, and Philip held up his hand, signaling a temporary cease-fire. The butler arranged everything before her in his usual efficient way, then poured her a cup of steaming hot coffee.

"Thank you, Barton," she murmured, and waited until he had gone back into the house to begin again. "The last thing in the world I want is your sympathy or your pity, Philip."

He eyed her levelly. "Relax. I don't feel sorry for you, but I am concerned. And whether or not you agree, I think a little concern is normal under the circumstances. One way or another, whether we like it or not, we're a part of each other's lives. Even if it's only that we're part of the same family. Even if it's only that you own stock in my company." He paused. "Can you understand that?"

Reluctantly she nodded. "I suppose so."

He silently congratulated himself on being able to present how he felt in such a relatively impersonal, unemotional way when what he really wanted to do was wrap her in silk batting to make sure she was never hurt again. And it was totally natural that he feel that way, he told himself. "Good. We agree on something. It's a start."

Her eyes narrowed. "A start?"

He smiled. "Lighten up, Jacey. It's just an expression."

He was telling *her* to lighten up? The man who had scowled at her every time he had seen her in the last ten years? "I need to ask a favor of you, Philip."

"Sure. What?"

"Please don't tell Mother about my illness."

"I think you're doing her an injustice by not telling her, but okay, I won't. Not if you don't want me to."

Tension she hadn't been aware of began to gradually ease. "Thank you. It's just that I'd rather not deal with her version of what I should or shouldn't have done."

"I won't say anything."

Maybe everything was going to be all right after all, she thought, picking up her coffee cup and taking a sip. Now that he knew she wasn't on drugs, and he had gotten over his anger that she hadn't had him notified, he seemed to be handling her illness pretty well.

Unfortunately, she had another problem. She didn't want to appear vulnerable or needy to him, but her reaction every time he kissed her made her feel *extremely* vulnerable and needy. She was definitely going to have to work on her resistance. Not that he would kiss her again. And not that she wanted him to.

From beneath the thickness of her lashes she watched him as he buttered a piece of toast. He managed to make worn jeans and a faded sweatshirt look both elegant and sexy, she thought ruefully. He could make a fortune giving lessons on how to do that. "Are you taking the day off?"

He shook his head. "No, I'm going into the office for a few hours. I've decided to call an unofficial stockholder meeting next week, and I want to get some statistics together. I hope I can convince everyone to stick with me."

"Why have the meeting unofficial?"

"Because there are only about twenty people who hold a sizable amount of the stock, and I want to concentrate on them. I know most of them personally. You know a lot of them yourself. They were old cronies of Dad's." He grimaced. "I'm afraid that I'm going to have a hell of a time getting them to come. The minute they receive my invitation, they'll know that I'm going to try to strong-arm them into staying with me and the company. I wouldn't be surprised if they immediately call their nearest travel agent to book a flight out of town."

"I don't understand. Why would you have to try to strong-arm them?"

"They're old guard, and, as I said, they were Dad's friends. The board might have offered the job of president to me, but at that point no one knew what I had in mind for the company. I came in and immediately started making changes, and pretty sweeping ones at that." The memory made him grin. "Believe me, I put more than a few noses out of joint. I know for a fact that many of the stockholders feel I'm now getting my well-deserved comeuppance."

His grin lingered, and she stared at his mouth. He had been talking about a serious, important subject, but suddenly all she could think about was how he had tasted when he kissed her yesterday. It was ironic, she thought. He had been worried about her being hooked on drugs, but in her opinion, his kisses were more dangerous and more addictive than any drug known to man. It would be easy for someone to allow him to become an obsessive habit. For *someone,* but not for her.

At that moment Barton walked out of the house carrying her breakfast, and she gave silent thanks for the distraction. She wasn't used to this fairly pleasant side of Philip, and she found this new mood slightly unnerving. But, she reminded herself, she had come home wanting to establish a cordial relationship with him, and now she had the opportunity.

"Thank you, Barton," she murmured as he finished serving her.

"Jacey." Edith hurried out of the house, the portable phone in her hand. "Dr. Milford is on the phone for you. He says he has the results of your test for you. What test? What is he talking about?"

Jacey's heart sank. Dr. Milford was also her mother's doctor, and she was sure when he had identified himself, her mother had asked him why he was calling her. Luckily it sounded as if he had been discreet. "Let me take his call, and then I'll explain."

She reached for the phone, already editing the truth so that she could come up with a story that wouldn't alarm her mother. She just hoped Philip would back her up.

"Dr. Milford? This is Jacey." As she listened to the doctor, her gaze drifted to Philip. He was watching her intently, just as her mother was. She felt as if two high-intensity lamps had been turned on her. "Thank you, Dr. Milford. I appreciate you calling." She punched the Off button and laid the phone down.

"Well?" Edith said.

She glanced at Philip, then back at her mother. "It's really nothing. You're already aware that I've been feeling a little tired since I've been back. Well, the day I went to have lunch with Bryan, I also went to see Dr. Milford. He ran a blood test, and as he told you, he was calling me with the results."

"What were they?" Philip asked casually.

She heard the edgy undercurrent in his tone and hoped her mother hadn't. "Just what the doctor and I thought they would be. There's nothing wrong. I've simply been traveling too much."

Edith's hand flew to her heart, and she made a sound of relief. "Thank goodness. For a minute there, I was really worried."

Jacey's eyes locked with Philip's. "There's nothing to worry about."

He stared at her silently, and she held her breath, wondering if he would give her away.

Then he sat forward and nodded toward an empty space at the table. "Why don't you join us for breakfast, Edith? It's a beautiful morning to be outside."

Edith looked extremely pleased and took the chair he indicated. "Thank you. I'd love to. Jacey darling, I'm so glad you decided to stay with us for a while. Even if there is nothing wrong with you, you obviously needed a good rest, and I have to say, you're looking much better than when you first arrived."

Jacey smiled. "Thank you for the compliment, Mother."

Somewhat to Jacey's surprise, the breakfast turned out to be quite enjoyable. The air was crisp and clear and filled with the smell of dried leaves and blooming chrysanthemums. Philip set out to be charming to both her and Edith, and though she knew he was doing it to make her mother happy, she also allowed herself to relax and appreciate his effort. It was alarmingly easy for her to bask in the glow of his attention.

Sometime later Edith placed her napkin beside

2

IN THE HEAT OF THE NIGHT • 115

her plate. "I better get my day started. I want to do a little shopping. I'd like to find something special to wear tonight."

"What's happening tonight?" Jacey asked idly.

"I'm going out with . . ." Edith's words trailed off and a flush of embarrassment stained her cheeks.

"With?" Jacey prompted, her curiosity pricked.

"With Robert Gage. We're going to the club. Well . . . several of us are. It's sort of a group thing." Edith pushed back her chair and stood. "You know how it is."

Jacey wasn't sure she did. "Robert Gage? Isn't he that man who—"

"Yes, yes, he is. Umm, well, I'll see you both later. Have a nice day."

Jacey gazed after her mother's hastily retreating figure. "What do you suppose that was about?"

Philip grinned. "I haven't got a clue, but I suppose I'd better get going too. Are you going upstairs to rest?"

"No. I think I'll take a walk down by the river."

His brows drew together with concern. "Do you think you should?"

"Sure. Why not? The exercise will do me good. I need to rebuild my stamina, and walking will help. I walked for over an hour at the plant yesterday before I started feeling tired." She looked down at the dog. "Maybe Douglas will come with me." Douglas opened one eye and glared at her. She smiled. "Then again, maybe not. Apparently he's reached his limit of exertion for the day."

Instantly, Philip changed his plans. "I'll come with you." He didn't like the idea of her being alone and out of sight of the house. She needed to be where people could take care of her and help her if she needed it.

"I thought you were going into the office," she said, surprised.

"I still plan to, only now I'll do it after our walk."

Her heart began to thud slowly. Philip was actually putting off work to spend time with her. Sternly she pulled herself together. It meant nothing. She slowly nodded. "Okay, then. It'll give me an opportunity to talk to you. I have an idea about the stockholder meeting you're planning."

He rose and held out his hand to her. In spite of her effort to remain levelheaded, his gesture made her heartbeat speed up. She took his hand and allowed him to draw her to her feet, but then she pulled her hand back to her side. However innocent his intention might be, it would be impossible for her to keep her mind on her idea if he was holding her hand.

They headed down the slope of the lawn toward the river, leaves occasionally crunching beneath their feet. When Douglas saw that Philip was going on the walk too, he lurched upright and lumbered after them.

"You said you had an idea?" he prompted when they were on the path that ran parallel to the river.

She nodded, unsure how he would take her suggestions or if he would welcome her involvement. He was being nice to her because he knew how ill she had been, but where KillaneTech was concerned, he might not be as nice. "What did you have planned for your informal shareholders meeting?"

He shrugged. "Planned? Nothing other than to invite them to my office one day next week and give them my viewpoint."

"And you said some of them would be reluctant to come?"

His mouth twisted into a wry grin. "There's no

doubt about it. Most of them have already decided to sell once the stock climbs a little higher. On the other hand, as I told you, some of them are relishing my difficult position and will probably show up just for the pleasure of seeing me sweat."

"Then why not turn the meeting into a social affair? Invite the men, along with their wives, here to the house for cocktails and dinner."

He looked at her oddly. "What would that accomplish?"

"For one thing, it would make it harder for them to refuse. We'll send the invitation to their homes so that their wives will see the invitations first."

"We?"

"Me. I'll arrange everything."

He shook his head. "No. Arranging a party would be too much work for you."

She smiled, warming to her idea. "Don't be such a mother hen, Philip. Addressing twenty invitations isn't going to put that much of a strain on me, and I'll have Barton and Mother to help me do the rest."

"I don't know. . . ."

The more she thought about the idea, the more enthusiastic she became. She placed her hand on his arm, bringing him to a stop. Douglas took the opportunity to plop down on the path for a little rest.

"Don't you see, Philip? The invitation will have greater impact if it comes from both of us. I'm sure they're aware that you've had my proxy all these years. Unfortunately that proxy was a great indicator of my disinterest. But at the party I'll make sure they learn that I'll be voting my own stock from now on, and that I think enough of what you've done and your plans that I'll be voting with you. They're bound to know that we've never been close and that I wouldn't have made an active decision to become involved unless I trusted you completely. Together we'll be presenting a unified front, and our solidarity can't help but build their confidence."

He shook his head again. "I don't like the idea of you doing all that work."

"For heaven's sake, Philip, pay attention. It won't be that much work, and this is a great idea. During the cocktail hour we'll load them onto a bus that has a bar and a bartender and—"

"A bus?"

"A bus. And we'll take them over to the plant so that you can show them what you showed me yesterday. Only limit the tour to the highlights; an hour is plenty. They'll be sold."

His jaw was set into a stubborn line. "It will never work."

"Why not? I was sold in the first five minutes, and they will be too. It will give them a chance to see the plant in a more personal light, not just as a piece of paper that indicates they own shares of stock or as a line on the stock exchange graph." She stared past him to the river, thinking. "We'll ask them to arrive at six. At six-thirty we'll load them onto the bus. Twenty minutes there, twenty minutes for the return. An hour there for the tour." She looked up at him and saw that he was scowling. "We should have them back here by eight-thirty easy, and have them sitting down to dinner eating the first course by nine. They'll be home by midnight. Perfect. What's wrong?"

"I don't like it." He knew he was being negative, but he couldn't stop himself. He was actually delighted that she was concerned about Killane-Tech and wanted to help. But he couldn't get the idea out of his head that she had nearly died—

that he had nearly lost her. He couldn't stand taking the risk that doing this might jeopardize her recuperation.

"Listen to me, Philip. Their wives will be eager to come to a dinner party here, and they'll think the trip to the plant is a great adventure."

"Adventure? Give me a break, Jacey."

"Trust me. Anything that's outside their normal everyday experience is viewed as an adventure. In California I once organized an evening at a biker's bar for a group of society's finest. Everyone had a great time."

Her eyes were sparkling, and a smile of enthusiasm graced her face. The fresh air had added more color to her cheeks, and the breeze had blown her hair into careless disorder. She resembled that young girl in the photograph in his office. It had been a long time since he had seen her this animated and excited, and he hated to spoil it.

He could feel himself softening.

The idea was a good one, a damned good one. *But* she was his wife, even if it was in name only, and he had a responsibility to her. Her health had to come first.

She tugged on his arm. "Come on, Philip. Admit it. It's a wonderful idea."

"It's not a bad idea," he said cautiously.

She laughed, a sound that wrapped itself around his heart with warmth. What was happening to him?

"Thank you, I think."

"Okay, it's a good idea. It's just too much work for you."

Her smile faded. "Philip, I promise you, if you insist on treating me like an invalid, I won't be responsible for my actions."

The warning tone in her voice had the hair on the back of his neck prickling. "What would you do?"

She thought about it. "Scream out of pure frustration, then most likely pack up and leave."

Ice slipped into his bloodstream. "You're not serious."

"Perfectly." She crossed her arms across her chest and eyed him steadily. "Why do you think I didn't want you and Mother to know? Because of the way you're acting now. I will *not* be treated as if I'm a child who doesn't know what's good for me."

He couldn't tell her that saving the company wasn't worth her risking a relapse or even worse. He couldn't tell her that he wouldn't be able to go on if she died. He couldn't tell her that he was still hopelessly and madly in love with her.

He whirled, putting his back to her, and squeezed his eyes shut. *Sweet heaven.* He was in *love* with her!

"Philip?"

"Give me a minute, Jacey. I need to think about your idea." What he needed was a psychiatrist. He *loved* her, but he knew with real certainty that his was a hopeless love, and he was in a dead-end situation. If he told her that he loved her, she really would leave. He knew there was no way she could ever love him in return, and though she had denied it, she might even hate him. She certainly had a right. Plus sooner or later he was going to have to face the fact that she would move on. Jacey never stayed in one spot too long.

But . . . if he let her get involved with the company, maybe, just maybe, he could keep her with him a little while longer.

"Philip? What's to think about? It's a good idea."

He turned back to her with a smile. "You're right. It's a wonderful idea."

"Then you'll let me do it? she asked, viewing his smile with caution. The smile had come from nowhere, and there was no telling what it meant.

"Yes."

Forgetting her caution, she impulsively threw her arms around his neck and hugged him. "You won't be sorry. I promise you won't."

Her warmth and perfumed scent engulfed him; the soft mounds of her breasts pressed into his chest; her pelvis rested against his lower body. "No," he said thickly, "I don't think I will be." Even if allowing her to plan the party gave him only another week with her, he wouldn't be sorry.

All at once she realized what she was doing and quickly broke away. "I—"

He placed a finger on her lips, stopping the words before she could utter them. "Don't apologize. Having you throw your arms around me is a nice change from having you throw daggers at me with your eyes."

"I've never done that."

He nodded. "Oh, yes, Jacey. You have. Each and every time you've seen me in the last ten years."

There was humor in his gaze and in his voice. And warmth. And something else. Whatever it was, she liked it, she decided. And they were now working together toward a common goal. The idea made her feel good. It also made her feel useful, something she hadn't felt in a long time.

By unspoken mutual agreement they continued with their walk, falling into step, side by side. With a long-suffering gaze at them, Douglas levered his bulk upward and trod after them.

"By the way," he said casually, "is there any

movie out on video you'd like to see? I thought I'd rent a few on my way home from work this evening, and we could watch them."

Surprise made her stumble.

His arm shot out to steady her.

"Movies would be fun," she murmured. "And get whatever looks good to you. It's been a long time since I've seen a movie, so anything you pick out will be fine."

He kept his arm around her waist. "I'll see what I can find."

Eight

Edith eyed the seating chart for the upcoming dinner party with the same absorption a general might use in studying a battlefield. "I think the Carmichaels should be separated—they bore each other to death. We'll put him by Meredith Danfield—she usually wears something low cut, and the view will keep him entertained. And we'll put Mrs. Carmichael by Randolph Olden—he has the uncanny ability to find even a discussion of root rot engrossing."

Jacey grinned with appreciation. "Whatever you think, Mother. You know these people far better than I do, and your instincts are impeccable. It's why I asked you to do the seating chart for me."

They were working at a table located at one end of the sitting room, going over the details for the party. Philip was also in the room, seated some distance away before the roaring fire he had lit to ward off the chill of the rainy day. Douglas snoozed while Philip studied a sheaf of documents and occasionally made use of the portable phone.

Jacey knew this because her attention kept straying to him.

A frown marred Edith's perfectly made up face. "I'm glad to do it, darling. In fact, I feel I should be doing more. Are you sure you don't want me to cancel my plans for that evening so that I can be here to help out?"

"Absolutely not. Everything will go beautifully." For Philip's sake, she fervently hoped her confident pose was justified. Privately, though, she had her doubts. She hadn't seen some of these people in years, the others she didn't know at all. Their reactions to the evening couldn't be guaranteed, no matter how thoroughly she planned. But as for herself, she was having a great time. It felt wonderful to be an active participant in life again instead of just an observer. And she supposed when all was said and done, all she could do was keep her fingers crossed and pray the evening went well.

"I'm sure everything will be perfect, but it's an important evening, and I would never have made these plans if I had known beforehand—"

"I know and I apologize for the short notice, but Philip and I decided to do this only five days ago. Besides, these plans of yours sound fun."

Edith laughed nervously. "Fun? It's just a driving tour of New England with a small group of friends to see the leaves."

Philip couldn't hear what Edith and Jacey were saying; because of the rain and the fire, their voices reached him as low murmurs. It should have made it easy for him to concentrate on the work he had brought home with him, but his attention kept wandering to Jacey. She seemed happier than he had seen her in a long time, he thought. She also looked as if she felt better. Her appetite had improved, along with her stamina, and her hours of sleep had been reduced to eight or nine hours at night and a couple of hours in the afternoon. He knew this because, very discreetly, he had been monitoring her every move.

Jacey's eyes twinkled. "Robert Gage wouldn't by any chance be involved in this little trip, would he?"

Edith's expression fell a trifle short of the severe look she was trying for. "Robert may be in the group I plan to meet up with. In fact, he may have even planned the whole thing. But I'm certainly not going out with him, as in having a *date*."

"Why not? You went out with him the other night."

"Just to the club. That doesn't count. Besides, I was maneuvered into it."

"Did you or did you not have a good time?"

Edith shifted as if her position had suddenly become uncomfortable. "Well, it wasn't exactly a bad time, but—"

"Mother, what's bothering you? I've never seen you so indecisive or vague about anything or anyone."

Edith rubbed her forehead. "It's this man. *Robert*. He simply won't take no for an answer. I've told him time and again that I'm not interested, but he just smiles, and then before I know what I'm doing, I've agreed to do something else with him."

"He sounds like an interesting man. I don't see the problem." On the other hand, she *did* have a problem. She had always been able to handle interesting men. Unfortunately for her, Philip wasn't just interesting, he was infinitely fascinating. She could feel his gaze on her, and from the way her nerves were tingling, he might have been touching her. She should be handling this better, she thought, angry at herself.

She didn't understand why she should feel so unsettled. Her goals were being achieved. She and her mother had actually managed to work together quite well on this party. Of course, she reflected wryly, her mother's preoccupation with Robert Gage had helped her out tremendously. But the way the harmony had been achieved wasn't important, only that it had been. And she and Philip had spent a lot of time together these last few days, amiably and congenially. If she felt tension in his presence, it was her own fault.

"Robert is so different from anyone I've ever known," Edith said, tearing a piece of paper into strips. "Take your father, for instance. He was a lovely man, but we were young, and he was caught up in building a career. Still, I loved him very much, and if he hadn't died, we would have been celebrating our thirtieth anniversary soon. But he did die, and you and I were left alone. Then in a few years Marcus came along." She smiled softly. "He was wonderful, but he, too, was totally involved in his career and his company. He was so dynamic, sometimes I felt as if I were caught up in a cyclone. He left me breathless, but I loved him so much." She paused for a moment, thinking. "And now there's Robert. He's easygoing and funny—he actually makes me laugh—and he seems to have all the time in the world to pursue me. I'm even beginning to suspect that he decided to join the club and move some of his business interests up here only after he met me." She threw up her hands, her expression one of complete bewilderment.

Jacey's mouth curved wryly. "He sounds like every woman's dream."

"But he— Oh, dear, what have I torn up?"

"Nothing important, and quit trying to analyze this thing with Robert to death. Take what's happening at face value. Apparently he's reached the point in his life when he doesn't have to spend too much time chasing after career goals because he's already achieved them. And so now he's obviously very smitten with you and is chasing you. I think it's great. If Mr. Gage has the good sense to pursue you, then he must be a terrific man."

Edith's brow wrinkled and she sighed. "I don't understand men."

Jacey tossed her hair behind her shoulder and laughed. Out of the corner of her eye she saw Philip's head come up. She lowered her voice. "Join the club, Mother. You're not alone." Understanding Philip would take a lifetime, she thought, and why would she want to anyway? Her goal of becoming his friend was coming true. That was enough, wasn't it? "Anyway, I'd say you've done pretty well in your life. You've had two great loves, and there are a lot of woman who have never even had one."

The phone rang, and Philip answered it.

Edith smiled at Jacey. "That's true, and you're one of those women."

Jacey stiffened. "We were talking about *you*, Mother, not me."

"I know, but I want so much for you to be happy, Jacey. It's what I've always wanted." Edith reached across the table and took her hand. "I know I'm hard on you sometimes, and if I've hurt you, I'm sorry. The thing is, I was terrified when your father died, terrified that I would make some awful mistake in raising you, and that somehow he would know and never forgive me. But I do love you, Jacey.

Unfortunately, being a mother has never come easily to me."

It was an apology and a reaching out to her. And it had taken an unusual combination of nonrelated events to make it happen: She had nearly died and had decided to come home, KillaneTech was in trouble and she and her mother had worked on a party together, and, helping matters along, her mother had fallen in love with a man from Oklahoma.

However it had happened, Jacey was very happy. With misty eyes she squeezed her mother's hand and smiled. "What you've just said means the world to me."

Philip saw the radiant smile spread across Jacey's face. His hand tightened around the phone, and, distracted, he pressed the button that disconnected the call. He would have given the world to have her smile at him like that, he thought.

"You know, darling," Edith said, "at one time I thought, I hoped—in fact both Marcus and I did— that you and Philip would fall in love."

Jacey started and cast a guilty glance at Philip. He was watching her. "You *did*?"

Edith nodded. "Marcus and I used to talk about it all the time. It was obvious that you had a crush on Philip, and we were hoping that once you came of age, that crush would develop into love and that he would grow to love you too."

With great deliberation Jacey shuffled the lists before her. "I guess some things aren't meant to be. Now, let's see . . . would you mind going over the dinner menu with me? I want to make sure it's absolutely right." She had few doubts about the menu, but she felt it was imperative to change the subject before she said or did something that would give her away.

There had been a time when she had loved Philip with all her young heart. And she would be dishonest if she didn't admit that there had been times in the past ten years when, in the darkness of some long, lonely night, she had yearned for him. But he had never loved her, and there was no point in yearning for what had never been and could never be. Instead, she needed to be content with the new, budding friendship that was developing between them. She needed to, but whether she could or not remained an open question.

"Miss Killane?"

Jacey glanced up from the magazine she had been reading to see Barton standing in the sitting room doorway. It was the evening before the party. Her mother was out, and Philip hadn't come home yet. "Yes, Barton?"

"The clothes from Marsha Cole's have arrived. I've had them placed in Mr. Killane's study. I also took the liberty of placing a dressing screen and a cheval mirror in there."

Marsha Cole was the name of a top dress store Philip had contacted earlier in the week, requesting that they send a selection of evening wear to the house for her. He had told her he had done it because he didn't see any sense in her tiring herself out, shopping for something to wear to the party. Since it was the only thing he had done or said all week to indicate that he was still concerned about her health, she decided she really couldn't complain. "Why did you have the dresses placed in the study?"

"Mr. Killane isn't home, and it seemed a likely,

out-of-the-way place. But if you'd rather I have them put somewhere else, I'll be glad to."

She was surprised to hear the barest hint of censure in Barton's tone, denoting he felt his choice had been not only the obvious one, it had been the correct one, and that it was possible she was a little dimwitted to be questioning him. "No, no, the study will be fine. Uh, thank you, Barton."

She put down the magazine and made her way into the study. A rack stood to one side of the room, filled with dresses—*ten* dresses, she discovered, after she had counted them. She hadn't expected so many to be sent, but her interest sharpened.

It had been a long time since she had been able to enjoy clothes and have fun finding that perfect something to wear that would help her look and feel great. The gorgeous clothes before her were hard to resist, and the upcoming party provided her with the perfect excuse to try to look her best.

She passed by a couple of basic black outfits and went on to a green plaid taffeta strapless number with a flirty little skirt. Too young looking, she thought. She considered a multicolored beaded jacket with a white chiffon skirt. Mentally she stamped it too conventional for her taste, but it would probably be appropriate for the party. A teal silk evening suit caught her eye, and she decided to come back to it after she had seen all the dresses. She stopped at a long, iridescent silver lace dress held together by tiny straps across the shoulders and back. It was beautiful, she thought, but—

"I like that one," Philip said.

She swung around to find him standing in the doorway. "I didn't know you were home."

"I just got here." He nodded toward the dress. "Are you going to try it on?"

She glanced over her shoulder at the dress. "I don't think so."

"Why not? It was made for you. Sophisticated and sexy."

Days ago he had compared her to a glacier. Now he saw her as sophisticated and sexy. It was a definite improvement, although she didn't agree with him. "It's too . . . uh . . . I'll have Barton move these things up to my room."

He walked in and shut the door behind him. "Don't bother. They're not in my way."

"No, I think I'd better have him move them. I'm sure he wouldn't have put them in here in the first place if he had known you were coming home so soon."

He took off his suit jacket and dropped into the chair behind his desk. "He knew. I called him to let him know I was on my way."

"You did? Then I don't understand why he had them put in here."

"I don't either, but it doesn't matter. Try the dress on."

"Now? With you here?"

Relaxed and at ease, he swiveled his chair back and forth. "Why not? You can go behind the screen. I'd like to see you in a couple of the outfits. After all, tomorrow night is important to me."

She couldn't argue with him there, she thought, and was unable to come up with an excuse that she *could* argue with him about. She returned to the dress rack. Deliberately passing up the silver lace dress, she pulled a short gold frock from the rack. Its sleeveless top was encrusted with sequins and beads, and the skirt that would end just above her knee was made up of three tiers of silk organza.

"It's nice," Philip drawled, loosening his tie and unbuttoning the top buttons of his shirt, "but I'd like to see the silver lace on you."

It *was* a dream of a dress, she thought, gazing at it. The kind of dress designed to make a woman feel glamorous, beautiful, and seductive. She *did* want to try it on. So . . . why not?

She replaced the gold dress on the rack, and with the lace dress went behind the screen. As quickly as she could, she stripped down to her panties and slipped into the dress.

Looking at herself, she realized what she had been trying to say about the dress. It was too *bare*. The neckline and back dipped precariously low, but the bottom of the dress was rather interesting with its small train. Since she wasn't wearing high heels, it pooled on the floor around her feet, as if she were a little girl playing dress-up in her mother's clothes.

Nervous and quite sure she looked ridiculous, she walked around the edge of the screen and, self-consciously, spun in a circle. "Here it is. Awful, isn't it? And I would definitely need a slip."

Philip's breath caught in his throat. The lines of her body were clearly visible beneath the lace. Her skin gleamed like liquid gold, and her breasts mounded alluringly high above the edge of the neckline. She looked as if she were wearing a shimmering silver cobweb.

Slowly, as if pulled by an unseen force, he rose and walked to her.

Arrested by the strange light that glittered in his eyes, she stopped tugging at the neckline and watched him come toward her. "Philip?"

"I like it," he said huskily, coming to a halt in front of her.

"I don't think this dress will do for tomorrow night," she murmured, extremely aware of the heated tension that had suddenly begun to build between them. "My presence is supposed to help the stockholders gain a feeling of stability, not insubstantiality." As an attempt at humor, her remark fell way short of the mark.

He didn't seem to notice. "How does it fit?" he asked, reaching out and skimming a finger beneath one fragile strap to the smooth skin of her shoulder.

She froze, afraid to even draw a breath. "Fine."

He hooked the finger around the strap and tugged at it. "This isn't too tight?" Mutely she shook her head. "Because I wouldn't want it to dig into your skin."

"It doesn't." To her dismay, she found that her throat had become constricted, making her words sound choked.

He pulled the strap off her shoulder and released it, then smoothed a finger back and forth over her bare shoulder where the strap had been. Staring down with brooding intensity, he murmured, "Your skin is so fine, so delicate—you bruise easily."

She should pull the strap back to her shoulder, duck behind the screen, and put her clothes back on. It was what she should do, but it wasn't what she wanted to do. She was mesmerized by his absorption with her and the dress, and she was mesmerized by him.

His hand lifted to the neckline and grasped its edge. As he did, the backs of his fingers brushed over her breast. "This is low, isn't it?"

She cleared her throat, but her answer still came out as a whisper. "Yes."

He nodded, his gaze focused on where his hand was. "The material looks as if it were made out of moon rays, but it has a texture to it. Is it scratching your skin?"

"No." Heat had welled up and congested in her chest until every breath she drew was filled with heat.

With a frown of concentration he delved deeper inside the neckline until the tips of his fingers nearly reached her nipple, feeling and testing the material for himself, and at the same time her.

The heat spread throughout her insides and quickly settled in her lower body, where it throbbed and pulsed. Her knees felt as if they might give way at any moment.

He flexed his fingers against her. "You are so soft . . . so damned soft. You should have only the smoothest and softest of materials against your skin. Silk, satin, velvet . . ."

"Philip—"

His finger scraped across her nipple and back again. She closed her eyes and swayed as desire, like a raging fire, engulfed her. She didn't know what he was thinking or even *if* he was thinking. But if he was waiting to see if she would stop him, she was afraid he was in for a long wait. She couldn't. The feelings swirling through her were impossible to fight. A part of her over which she had no rule wanted them to go on and on. . . .

"Have you begun divorce proceedings yet?" he asked hoarsely.

She opened her eyes and found herself staring straight into his. Naked want was etched in his face, and she could feel herself begin to tremble. Her heartbeat and her heart were out of control.

"I know you haven't been into the city to see your lawyer this week," he said, his breathing ragged, "but you might have called him and told him to begin. Have you?"

She opened her mouth, but no sound came out. She mouthed the word no.

"So we're still married . . ." Primitive satisfaction showed in his eyes, his tone, and the stance of his body.

His finger continued to stroke back and forth over her nipple. She gave up trying to answer him, and instead watched his lips as they moved, speaking to her.

". . . and it's been ten years since we had that one night."

His fingers fastened onto her nipple and tugged. She gave a small cry that sent fire to his hardened groin. "Do you know that I still remember what you taste like?"

She had closed her eyes again. Her lashes lay in a silky, feathery shadow over her cheeks, and her head drooped, like a lovely flower on a delicate stem. He had never seen her more lovely or desirable. Suddenly he couldn't take it anymore. He dipped his hand into the neckline of the dress and took the full weight of her breast into his hand, bent his head, and pulled the nipple into his mouth. Sweetness and heat suffused his entire being, but it wasn't enough.

He wrapped his arm around her waist and lifted her so that he could have better suction. He tugged and pulled and sucked on her, trying to get ten years' worth of her all at once. And he was frustrated in his effort. He couldn't get enough of her.

Feelings of pure ecstasy pounded through her. She put her hands on his shoulders for balance, but that was an instinctive action, not a thinking one. She was all emotion, all desire. The bodice of her dress had fallen down, and when he switched his mouth to her other nipple, a sound of intense satisfaction welled up from the depths of her soul.

She tasted like heaven to him, and the thought raced through his mind that if he died right at that moment with her nipple in his mouth, he would be happy. He was thinking insane, acting insane. But crazed as he was, he knew he had to stop. Somehow. Some way.

He slowly lowered her, sliding her down his body, rubbing her over his hardened desire, reveling in the last bit of painfully exquisite pleasure.

When her feet touched the floor, he held on to her a little longer, unable to let her go just yet. And he kissed her again, filling her mouth with his tongue just as he wanted to fill her body with himself. She clung to him, the dress below her breasts, her pointed nipples thrusting into his chest through the cloth of his shirt. No woman had ever been able to fire his blood as she did, no woman had ever been able to obsess him.

She might be his wife, but she had never been his. The thought had him slowly lifting his head. "Can you stand?"

Without knowing whether she could or not, she nodded.

He released her and took a step away from her. His chest hurt as he drew deep breaths in and out of his lungs, trying to clear his brain.

"I want you," he said roughly, "but I know you don't want me . . . and I won't take advantage of you."

A thrill shot through her. He *wanted* her. Lord

knew she wanted him. If the truth were known, she had always wanted him. But where exactly did that leave them? she asked herself as she stood there aching for him, yearning to wrap her arms around his neck and pull him back to her.

It left them nowhere.

Philip was being infinitely wiser and more sensible than she, and she understood why. They both remembered a night when he hadn't pulled away, when he had gone ahead and given in to what they both wanted and had made love to her. The lovemaking had been fantastic, but the aftermath was a disaster. She might have loved him that night, but he didn't love her, and they had both suffered grief because of it. Neither one of them needed a repeat of the same situation.

Wrapping her arms around herself to try to stop the trembling, she went behind the screen and changed back into her clothes.

The next evening Jacey chose the gold dress to wear. It wasn't as spectacular as the silver, but it was lovely in its own right. And unlike the silver dress, it didn't hold the memories of the previous night, when she would have willingly and foolishly given herself to Philip.

Going downstairs to check on last-minute details, she reminded herself for the hundredth time that Philip had been right to pull away from her. Somehow it didn't make her feel any better.

Pausing in the dining room before the table that was already set, she heard a niggling voice in her head. If they made love again, it wouldn't be the *exact* same situation as their one night together. She had loved him then, but she didn't love him now. It might make spending another night in his arms easier. On the other hand, it might very well make it worse.

She shook her head. No. It couldn't be.

They might want each other, but they had both learned the hard way that wanting wasn't enough. She needed to do something to ensure that what had happened the previous night wouldn't be repeated. Now that she was physically much better, there was no reason why she shouldn't return to her apartment in the city and begin to make a new life for herself, a life without the constant traveling, a life that would involve seeing both her mother and Philip only on an occasional basis. She felt a pang in the region of her heart and determinedly ignored it. Yes, she decided. She would leave in the next day or two.

A few minutes later her mother found her making minor adjustments to the dining table centerpiece. "I've come to say good-bye. Oh, darling, you look beautiful, just beautiful. That dress was a perfect selection. It covers your collarbone and doesn't show how thin you are."

Jacey smiled wryly. Her mother would never change completely, but she understood her a little better now and she was happy with the new friendship they had begun to forge. "Thank you, Mother. You look lovely too."

Edith nervously fiddled with the scarf at her neck. "I wasn't quite sure what to wear. Robert is sending a car for me. Those of us who are going on the trip are meeting at the club, then we're going to caravan into the city, but we won't get a chance to change before the play tonight."

"A play? How nice. You'll enjoy that. By the way, I've been meaning to tell you that you're welcome to stay at my apartment. Say the word, and I'll give you the key."

Edith examined her nails. "That won't be necessary. Robert has taken a block of rooms at a hotel for everyone."

Jacey arched one eyebrow. "That will be convenient."

Edith caught the glint of humor in her daughter's eye. "I said for *everyone*."

"I know. I heard."

Edith nervously fiddled with the scarf at her neck. "You know it's not too late. I could still change my plans and stay home. You might need some help."

Jacey laughed and took her mother's hands in hers. "I never knew you were such a coward. You know as well as I do that I don't need your help, Mother."

"But—"

"The only thing you've got to do is concentrate on relaxing and having a great time."

Edith cleared her throat, then sighed. "Yes, I'm sure you're right. All right, then." She glanced at her watch. "I'd better have Barton collect my luggage. The car should be here any minute." She gave Jacey a quick hug. "You've done a superb job, darling. There's not a doubt in my mind that tonight will go just as you want it to."

"Thanks. For Philip's sake, I hope it will."

Nine

"What happened to the silver dress?"

The crystal vase full of fresh flowers almost slipped from Jacey's hands. Carefully she placed the vase on a side table and turned to face Philip, who was wearing a black evening suit set against a white shirt. The combination enhanced the darkness of his skin, hair, and eyes, and the whiteness of his teeth. His every pore exuded magnetism and sex appeal, and the very air around him seemed electric. In her own mind she didn't see how anyone could refuse him anything, but then, she reminded herself, the stockholders weren't as susceptible to him as she was. She was sure no one in the world was.

"I sent it back along with the others."

"It's just as well. As you said, it wasn't really appropriate for this evening." And there was no way he would have been able to keep his mind on business if she had worn the silver dress, he reflected grimly. As it was, he was going to have a hell of a tough time. She had chosen the gold dress with its glittering beaded top and flower petal–like silk organza skirt. She looked stunningly beautiful and every inch a lady, exactly right for tonight's function. And he had a strong urge to tear the dress from neck to hem, bare her slim body to him, and make love to her until neither one of them could remember the present, much less the past.

With a silent curse he jerked his gaze from her and did a quick survey of the salon where the evening would begin for their guests. He found what he was searching for—the bar—and headed for it.

"Are you nervous?" she asked, watching him reach for the Scotch bottle.

"*Terrified* would be a more apt description." He poured himself a shot of the whiskey and downed it.

"Terrified? You?"

He gave a short laugh. "What's the matter, Jacey? Don't you believe I'm capable of feelings?"

What she believed about him was complicated, and if she hadn't been able to sort it out in ten years, she certainly wouldn't be able to in the short amount of time they had before their guests arrived. "Everything's going to be fine, Philip. You'll see."

The whiskey burned its way through him but offered little help. The knots in his stomach had never been tighter or hotter. He wondered at the cause, how much was due to what would happen tonight with the stockholders and how much was because of Jacey. He looked at her for a minute longer, and all the while he felt the knots twist and tangle. He reached a conclusion. *The cause was Jacey.*

He strolled back to her. "If tonight works, it will

be because of you. I can't thank you enough for everything you've done."

"I enjoyed it," she said with a smile.

Her eyes glinted with warmth, something he wouldn't have thought possible days earlier, something he would like to see for a long, long time to come. She still held much of herself in reserve, but by volunteering to help him with this evening, by saying she would vote her stock his way, she had aligned herself on his side. He knew he shouldn't place too much importance on her actions, but where she was concerned he was a desperate man, reaching for straws. Unfortunately, as everyone knew, straws were too flimsy to hold on to.

He eyed her reflectively. "Your stock would probably be worth more if the company was taken over. Have you thought of that?"

Her smile broadened. "Are you trying to talk me out of this?"

"Not by a long shot. The company is really all I have, but you should think about what's best for you."

How sad, she thought, to hear him say that the company was all he had. It didn't seem right. A man like him should have so much, a wife who loved him, children . . . But it hadn't happened—for either of them.

And in spite of his feeling as he did about the company, he was still concerned about her. She was touched. "I *am* thinking about what's best for me. Marcus would come back and haunt both of us if we let his company fall into unfriendly hands."

He grimaced. "He may anyway, or at least me. Wherever he is, I'm sure he's calling me a damned fool for putting his business in jeopardy."

"You haven't lost yet," she said softly.

Impulsively, compulsively, he gently brushed his hand down the side of her face where the sequins and beads of her dress were reflecting light onto her skin. "I lost a long time ago, Jacey."

"What do you mean?"

He shook his head. "I shouldn't have said anything. Besides, it's nothing for you to worry about."

The doorbell rang. He smiled down at her. "It's show time. Are you ready?"

She nodded, still pondering his remark. Was it possible he had regrets about what had happened between them ten years ago? The idea rocked her to her toes. It was like someone trying to convince her it was midnight when she was staring straight at the sun. She couldn't believe it.

But if there was the remotest possibility he did have regrets . . .

They had never faced what had happened that night, how they had felt about it, and how it had affected their lives. Maybe they'd both feel better if they talked about it together, got everything out in the open.

Yet something like that could be dangerous. Out in the open, all the suppressed hurt and heartbreak might well up like a tidal wave and crash down on top of them, destroying not only the fragile relationship that had formed over the last week, but them as well.

Philip stood with Mr. and Mrs. Orson Caswell, nodding pleasantly. He knew that Orson Caswell was one of his staunchest adversaries and was waiting to sell his stock until it reached a certain price. There was no way the two of them could have had a civil meeting in the boardroom. Yet here the two of them were, smiling at each other, while Mrs. Caswell regaled him with the details of their latest trip to the Orient. Jacey had definitely known what she was doing when she had suggested this party. No one had declined their invitation.

As surreptitiously as possible, he kept track of her as she moved from one group to the next. It was fascinating to watch her in action. With a gesture, a smile, and a few words, she managed to make each man feel as if he were the most important, most intelligent person in the room. And at the same time, she somehow conveyed to each woman that she was the cleverest and most beautiful. It was an art, and she was practicing if for him.

His heart expanded with love, and even the unhappy knowledge that she was doing it only because of some sense of family obligation and not because she loved him changed nothing. He continued to watch and want her and silently applaud her.

When the time came, Jacey herded everyone on board the bus, and almost before they knew what was happening, they were on the way to the plant. She had ensured the trip would be a continuation of the party by renting a bus that came equipped with a bar and a stereo system. Walking up and down the aisle, she joked and laughed with everyone, making sure the mood stayed festive, until Philip began to worry about her.

The next time she passed him, he pulled her down into the vacant seat beside him. She had a smile on her face from a remark someone had made and her eyes were twinkling with merriment. It made him wish to heaven that they were alone.

"You're doing too much, Jacey. Take it a little easier."

Ignoring his admonition, she gaily laughed. "Things are going really well, aren't they?"

He resisted softening and giving into her good humor. He was crazy in love with her, and it was imperative that he watch out for her. "Yes, they are, but it will all come to a crashing stop if you collapse."

"Collapse? What are you talking about? I'm fine." She leaned toward him with a conspiratorial air. "I saw you talking to the Caswells. How did you do with them?"

His mouth twisted wryly. "They're a mismatched pair. He's about as easy to engage in conversation as a rock, and you can't stop her talking."

"This tour of the plant is going to swing things in your favor. You'll see." She craned her neck to look out the window. "Oh, great, we're nearly there. Are you ready?"

"I'm ready, but I need you to do something for me."

"Sure, what? Do you want me to take care of the Caswells for you?"

"I want you to take care of yourself. That way I can concentrate on what I have to do."

Her smile faded and her expression turned thoughtful. "Why would you worry about me? You shouldn't. You need to be thinking about what you're going to say to everyone once we're there."

"Make it easy for me," he said wryly. "Quit flitting around like a butterfly on speed. I keep thinking you're going to crash and burn any minute."

A reluctant smile tugged at her lips. "A butterfly on speed, huh? All right, all right, I'll do my best imitation of a turtle on tranquilizers. Will that make you happy?"

"Ecstatic."

"Great." She peered out the window again. "Well, we're here. This part of the evening is your baby. Good luck."

He finally allowed himself to soften. "I have a feeling I don't need luck with you on my side," he said huskily.

It was an odd thing for him to have said, Jacey reflected minutes later as she watched Philip begin the tour with a speech. He was grateful to her for helping him out, of course. He had said so many times this past week. But gratitude was where his feelings for her stopped, and she had to remember it. She would, she told herself. She definitely would. But she couldn't help but be proud of him as she listened to him speak to the group.

He laid out exactly what he had done and why, then went into his plans for the future, all in a clear, concise, and, most of all, persuasive manner. The employees working on the evening shift gathered around him, unobtrusively showing their respect and their support. He brought several of them forward to tell a little bit about themselves and what they thought about the changes he had made as it concerned them and their lives. Then he led the group on an abbreviated tour, saving the last fifteen minutes to allow his guests to wander wherever they chose and to talk with whomever they wished, without him being present.

The women enjoyed themselves immensely, meandering in their evening wear among the giant pieces of machinery, stopping here and there to strike up conversations with the employees, learning their names and if they had children and grandchildren. Some of them asked more technical questions, as did the men. And in the process, everyone learned why the employees had gained a new enthusiasm for working at KillaneTech.

It was a good tactic, because it presented the employees to the stockholders as real people with names and families instead of just faceless workers.

The wives beamed and the men mellowed.

Back at the house, the dinner, under Barton and Jacey's supervision, went like clockwork. The food and wine were superb, the conversation stimulating and fun.

By the time everyone left, Philip had gotten what he wanted: a stockholders' agreement signed by everyone present indicating their intention to hold on to their stock for two years, plenty of time for his plans to see fruition.

A fire blazed in the sitting room fireplace. Douglas, never one to let a good fire go to waste, was sprawled in front of it, snoring softly.

Jacey, on the other hand, was too keyed up to even think about sleeping yet. The success of the evening had excitement bubbling through her veins. *Together she and Philip had kept the business in the family.*

But Philip, slumped in a chair, staring at the stockholders' agreement in his hand, had reverted to his enigmatic self and didn't seem to be feeling the same satisfaction she was. He had taken off his jacket; his tie hung loose around his neck and his shirt was partly unbuttoned.

"You don't look very happy," she said speculatively. "I would have thought you would be jumping for joy. You got everything you wanted."

He tossed the document aside. He didn't have quite everything he wanted, he reflected, gazing at her, and the thought that he never would had him quietly losing his mind.

"I'm very pleased," he said. He was also aching for her with every muscle and joint of his body. He had just spent an evening watching her at her glittering, scintillating, and infinitely sexy best. He was sure more than one of the men, whether they were married or not, would dream about her that night. He knew he would. Hot, fiery, erotic dreams.

"Then what's wrong?"

"I'm just tired, that's all."

She grinned. "That's certainly a switch. Usually it's me who's tired."

He rose to his feet. "I think it's time I went upstairs, and you should do the same. If you're not tired now, you will be soon. It'll hit you like a delayed reaction."

She shook her head. "No, it won't. I'm too exhilarated. Stay with me, have a nightcap."

In spite of his well-meaning intentions, his pulse quickened. Jacey, in this mood, was like a bottle of champagne—golden, irresistible, and intoxicating. "I don't think so. I've had enough."

"You haven't had anything to drink since the Scotch before the party."

One dark eyebrow lifted. "You were keeping count?"

She had done much more than keep count, she thought. Nothing he had done had escaped her attention. She shrugged, admitting nothing. "Would you like a drink?"

"No."

"Then stay while I have a drink."

She was actually inviting him to be with her. He wished with all his heart that he could stay as she wanted and have a pleasant chat about the night's events. But he wanted to be with her in more than the casual way she had in mind, and he was afraid that if he stayed, he would say or do things that would make her turn her back on him forever.

"Do you drink?" he asked skeptically. "As far as I know, you haven't drunk anything alcoholic since you've been home, and I know you didn't have anything tonight."

Now it was her turn to raise a brow. "Keeping count?"

"Yes." Of her every breath. He was in danger of losing complete control. He could feel it in the very marrow of his bones.

An element of danger had penetrated the atmosphere around them, heightening and sharpening the excitement Jacey was feeling. A warning bell went off in her head, telling her she should back off from asking him to stay with her, but common sense seemed to have no part in her enthusiasm about the night's happenings. Her adrenaline was pumping, and after years of being alone and months of being sick, she wanted the good feelings to last as long as possible.

"Stay with me a little while longer," she said softly. "We don't have to drink. We could talk."

"I don't think that's a good idea."

The warning bell became louder, but she rushed blindly ahead, unsure where she was going, knowing only that she desperately wanted to get there. "You don't want to spend time with me?"

Pain shot into his jaw as he gritted his teeth. But when he spoke, there was no sign of his inner turmoil. His tone was calm, his words slow, his enunciation perfect. "The problem, Jacey, is that I do want to spend time with you."

"You want to but you won't?"

"I can't."

She could no longer ignore the warning bell. Tension had gathered in the air between them until it was almost impenetrable. Self-preservation instincts surged to the surface of her consciousness. She wasn't sure exactly what was happening, but it was most definitely time to retreat and regroup.

With a smile she spread her hands out, indicating that she was giving in. "All right then, maybe you're right. Maybe it is time to say good night." She paused, allowing herself just an extra few precious moments of time with him. "Philip?"

"Yes."

"I'm really happy for you." In a move even she couldn't have predicted, she suddenly rose on tiptoe and brushed her lips across his. "Good night."

The brush of her lips caused a searing along his nerves straight to his groin. His long fingers clamped around her upper arms like bands of iron. He looked down at her, his eyes dark with fire, his expression pained, his voice hoarse with longing. "I almost made it. I was almost able to let you get away, but then you had to go and kiss me."

"I'm sorry if—"

His hands tightened around her arms. Held captive in a hell of his own making, he didn't hear her. "I didn't want this to happen. I took advantage of you once. I didn't want to make the same mistake again, but now . . ." His gaze dropped to her mouth. Her lips were slightly parted as she took quick, short breaths. He was very much afraid that he was about to kiss her unless something happened to stop him.

"Philip, what— Are you talking about that night we spent together ten years ago?"

"You can't tell me you never think about it."

"I try not to." It was the truth, but she omitted telling him that she failed every time.

With a curse he released her, and with barely controlled violence he drove his hand through his hair. "Go to bed, Jacey. Forget what I just said."

They had been standing on the edge of something important, she realized, but he had backed away. "No, I think we should talk about it." She laid her hand on his arm, as if by doing so she could somehow make him listen to her and believe her. "You didn't take advantage of me all those years ago, Philip. *I* went to *you*, remember? And nothing happened I didn't want to happen."

His eyes were shadowed with a private anguish. "You were so young."

"Yes, I was. And in love." There. For the first time she admitted her love to him.

His lips firmed. "You had a crush on me, Jacey. You only *thought* it was love."

"You're right. I definitely thought it was love. In fact, I was convinced, and, I repeat, you weren't to blame."

Once again he wrapped his fingers around her upper arms, only this time he did it more gently. "But you didn't know what love was."

She had been absolutely convinced that she did, but if it had been love, surely it would have lasted, she thought. "Okay, I'll agree with you there. Apparently I didn't know, but my not knowing doesn't alter a thing."

"Do you know now what love is?" He wasn't sure

he wanted to hear her answer, but he was driven to ask.

"No." How could she? She had been running for the past ten years, avoiding all but the most superficial of relationships.

His expression turned grim, but his thumbs absently stroked the soft skin of her upper arm. "I shouldn't have brought the subject up."

Heat flared where he was touching her, spread down to her fingertips, and up to her brain. "Maybe it was good that you did," she murmured huskily. "It's there between us—the memories of that night."

"The memories are good, *too* good." He dipped his head and grazed his mouth across hers. He had done it, and now he wouldn't be able to stop. "They come back to me at the damnedest times, and I grow hard just remembering how sweet and wild you were that night." He pressed his mouth to hers lightly.

A fire started in her belly, and she swayed. He was in agony; she could hear it in his voice. He was struggling over his part in their past and with the fact that he wanted her in the present. Her heart thudded against her rib cage. And suddenly, clearly, she knew what she wanted.

"I shouldn't even touch you now," he said roughly, drawing back his head and gazing at her lips, then into her eyes.

"But you're going to," she said softly. "Please say you're going to."

His hand trembled as he raised it to her face. "Jacey, you don't have to say please to me. Just smile."

Her smile came slowly, spreading across her face, illuminating everything about her.

For a minute he could only stare, then he crushed his mouth down on hers with the force and desperation of a man whose willpower had just snapped in two.

He had resigned himself to long, dark, lonely years of loving her, but to never being able to have her. He had never once dared hope that he would get another chance to make love to her, but by her smile she had given her consent. She didn't return his love, but unknowingly, with her smile, she had asked him to give her his love, because when they came together, when he entered her, he would truly be making love to her. And if he were to have only this one chance, he was determined to try to make sure that they would both remember this night for the rest of their lives.

Deliberately forcing himself to slow down, he briefly lifted his head, then slanted his mouth back across hers in a different, somehow more erotic angle. He wrapped his arms around her and pulled her to him until he had her close against him. With his hand against her bottom he pressed her into him, locking their lower bodies together.

After all the days, weeks, and years of resisting him—even though the resisting had been just in her mind—Jacey allowed herself to relax and to savor what was happening. Her arms slid around his neck, her fingers wove up into the clean thickness of his hair. It was like a miracle to her to be able to freely touch him and kiss him and have him do the same to her in return. She had spent ten years trying to escape him, and now she wanted nothing more than to wrap her legs around his hips and hold him deep inside her.

But much to her growing frustration, he seemed to be in no hurry. His tongue made lazy, knowledgeable forays deep into her mouth, rasping against her tongue until her blood was rushing through her veins, hot and fast.

"Let's go upstairs," she whispered.

"In a minute." His voice was rough and husky, but his hands were gentle as they skimmed beneath her skirt to her thighs. His nails scored up and down one stocking, then he sought out the soft flesh of her inner thigh.

She gasped as heat crawled into her lower body, where it quickly formed into a pool of fire. Why were they waiting? It had been so long. . . . "Now?" she asked plaintively.

He shook his head. "Not yet." His fingers found the snaps of her lacy garter belt and flipped them open one by one.

Jacey felt her hose slide down her thighs and moaned with pleasure. Now, she thought. Now they would go upstairs. But suddenly his long fingers were beneath her panties, flexing into the soft skin of her buttocks, stroking and lightly pinching. Desire scored through her. She wrapped one leg around him and pushed her lower body against the hard cradle of his pelvis. "Now. Please . . ."

Without answering her he cupped her bottom, lifted her, and moved her up and down over his blatant masculine hardness. Aching with need for him, half crazy with the emptiness that throbbed inside her to be filled, she gave a small cry and threw her head back.

His legs threatened to give way. He had delayed going upstairs almost too long—he was already at the point where he was ready to take her there on the sitting room floor—but still he delayed.

Because he was afraid.

He didn't want their first time after so many years to be on a floor. He wanted to take her to bed, where he could luxuriate in each sensation and relish each new level of enjoyment as together they climbed higher and higher. But *could* he? He wanted her so badly, he was afraid he might climax the first time he thrust into her, and if he did, it wouldn't be good for her. He had to make a decision, or soon there would be no decision to make.

The decision came instantly and was born of desperation. He would take her upstairs, and if he didn't satisfy her this time, he would the next. And the next. They had all night. If he had his way, they were going to have the rest of their lives.

"Now," he muttered. He lowered her feet to the floor, but then almost immediately swung her up into his arms. He felt weak with need, and he didn't know if he had the strength to carry her up the stairs, but he also couldn't bear the thought of being physically separated from her for even a moment.

He carried her out of the room, and neither one of them noticed when one of her shoes dropped from her foot. It didn't cause Douglas any concern either. He opened his eyes, yawned, and went back to sleep.

Sleep was the last thing on Philip's mind. In his room, with the door closed against the outside world, he once more lowered her feet to the ground. Unzipping her dress, he managed an unsteady grin. "I know I should try to go slowly, but I don't know if I can. I'm so hot I may explode."

She shook her head, her blond hair shimmering as she did. "Don't go slow." She slipped the dress from her shoulders, and the heaviness of the beaded top carried the dress to the floor, where it lay like a glittering flower around her feet.

She stepped out of it, kicked off the remaining shoe, and whispered, "Hurry or *I* may explode."

He wanted her so much, he found it painful to move. Fear still gripped him that, after all these years, he would fail her in some way, but there was nothing he could do about that fear. He was caught up in the excruciating dilemma of wanting her too much.

He brushed her hair away from her face. "I want you to enjoy this. You were so innocent before. . . ."

Hardly aware of what she was doing, she lay down on the bed and held her arms out to him. "Hurry, Philip. I want to feel you inside me."

With a tortured groan he ripped open his shirt and stripped out of it. Unbuckling his belt, he flipped off his shoes and quickly maneuvered out of his pants and socks. Then at last he was standing before her, naked and proudly, fully, erect. Her eyes devoured him, and he felt the heat of her gaze on him everywhere. It was a sensation that ended what feeble resistance he still had left. He went down to her and was enfolded in her arms.

Knowing how much she wanted him somehow made it easier for him to pace himself. The panties, garter belt, and bra that she still wore were little more than wisps of lace and air. His muscles trembled, but his hands were amazingly sure as he carefully finished undressing her. Then they were both naked, and the shock of skin against skin was like an earthquake in his soul.

He leaned over and covered her mouth with his, and at the same time slid his fingers between her legs. Moist, inviting warmth greeted him. She opened her mouth beneath his, spread her legs, and with a small sound that came from the back of her throat, rotated her hips against his hand.

Fire ignited in his brain and in his groin. "Jacey, you're not even giving me a chance to do this right."

Amazingly, she laughed softly, huskily, at him, at herself. "There's no way you could do it wrong. I want you too much."

He came up over her and drove into her, burying his length to the hilt. She closed tightly around him, her muscles strong, her body willing and pliant. He was overwhelmed by her—by her scent, by her taste, by her slim, quivering body. He pounded into her like a man demented, and she met him thrust for thrust.

Any thoughts of luxuriating or relishing fled. His body was acting independently of his brain, and he was helpless to do anything but react to her wildness. She cried out his name, and he answered with hers. Passion at its fullest, most potent strength arced and zinged from him to her and back again. Instinctively they moved as one, knowing what the other needed.

A storm had been brewing in each of them for ten years; now joined together, the storm was at hurricane force. It raged and roared as raw, primitive need for each other assaulted them. Finally, incredibly, wondrously, the storm crested in him, in her.

Jacey stiffened as powerful waves of pleasure tore through her. She clung to him, sobbing. And he clung to her, sharing the intensity and the pleasure, holding her close, loving her with all his heart.

Ten

Now she knew what love was, Jacey thought, lying in the early morning light, listening to the man she loved breathe as he slept.

Philip.

Love was Philip.

She came up on one elbow and gazed down at him. He was lying on his side, his back to her. A small smile curved her lips. She had been so wrong to think that she no longer loved him. No matter what she had thought, no matter how hard she had tried, no matter how far she traveled, she had never stopped loving him.

She reached out a hand and lightly skimmed it along his side into the dip of his waist and over the strong, lean line of his hip. Even in repose, the strength of his muscles was evident. Last night those muscles had bunched and strained as he had taken her into a realm of pleasure that her previous one night with him hadn't begun to prepare her for. Those had been precious, never-to-be forgotten times when, joined, they had hung suspended above reality and had shared the fury and the passion of the storm. Then together they had plunged over the edge to be consumed by a fire so hot, they had melded and truly become one, sharing each other's breath and heartbeat.

It was deeply satisfying to her to know that he had received every bit as much gratification as she had. But she had no illusions that last night had changed anything basic between them. The earth, so to speak, might have moved for both of them, but he still didn't love her any more than he had ten years before.

The only difference this time was that they were older, more in control of their own lives. She hoped he wouldn't feel the guilt he had back then. And if by some odd chance he did, she would make it a point to quickly rid him of the notion. She didn't want him to feel he owed her anything.

Philip felt her fingers on him and fought against opening his eyes. If he was dreaming, he didn't want to wake; he wouldn't be able to bear it if he awoke and found she had fled once again.

But as her touch continued, and her light, gentle fingers sought out the lines and curves of his torso, his blood began to heat and his body began to respond. And it became imperative for him to wake up and join the dream in progress.

He rolled over on his back, and the first thing he saw was her eyes—warm, liquid aqua, mirroring his growing desire. A feeling of love rolled through him with an intensity that left him shaken.

Without a word she slid on top of him, fitting herself over him, gloving him deep inside herself. If last night was a fiery storm, the morning proved to be silken heat. But it was equally consuming, and the final release was even more powerful.

Jacey sat up and swung her legs over the side of the bed. "I'm going back to my room. I need to shower and change." They had been lying quietly side by side for several minutes, not touching, not talking.

He lay a hand on the smooth skin of her bare back, one finger in the indentation of her spine, idly stroking. "Why?" he asked huskily. "I like the way you smell."

She smelled of him and of the sex they had had, she thought. It was an erotic, musky scent that made her weak at the knees and yearn to crawl back into bed with him. She bent from the waist, dislodging his hand, and scooped her gold dress off the floor. "I like a shower first thing in the morning. It wakes me up."

"Then stay here, and we'll take a shower together."

An enticement of further ecstasy was implicit in his suggestion. For a split second she wavered. There was no doubt that the sex between them was extraordinary, and she supposed it could go on indefinitely. But with her at least, sex with Philip went beyond the physical. Her heart was deeply involved, and she needed time and distance to regroup and to decide if she could bear to settle for just sex with him whenever they happened to be in the same place at the same time.

She had opened herself to him in every way, and now she felt a real need to shield herself from him, even if it was only with fabric. She stood, slid the dress over her head, and immediately felt a little stronger. Without bothering to zip the dress, she turned back to him. She shouldn't have.

He was propped up against a pile of pillows, a white sheet pulled to his waist. Dark hair spread across his broad chest and ran down the center of his abdomen in a narrow line that disappeared beneath the sheet. But she didn't need to see beneath the sheet to know what was there. The image of his lower body was seared into her brain like a permanent picture. More hair curled at his groin. And his manhood . . . If she took the swelling that pressed against the sheet into account, she knew he would soon be ready for her again. She jerked her gaze away and swallowed to relieve the dryness of her throat.

"Jacey?"

"I have to get ready to go into town today. I have an appointment."

He sat straight up, his expression concerned. "With the doctor?"

"No. An old friend is in town. I'm having lunch with her."

"Her?" He silently cursed the suspicion that tinged his voice.

"Ashley Whitfield. Do you remember her?"

Relaxed again, he dropped back down against the pillows, his gaze thoughtful. "Yeah. Red hair. Pretty. A little crazy. Always getting lost."

She smiled at the description. "That's her. Well, she married Max Hayden and lives in California now, but she's here on a visit and I want to see her."

"When will you be home?"

She shrugged. "Later on this afternoon." She

was almost at the door when she remembered there was something she needed to say to him. She looked back at him. "I wanted last night, Philip, just as I wanted that night ten years ago. There's nothing for you to feel guilty about, *ever*, at least not about me." She walked out and closed the door after her.

He stared at the door, stunned. And anger began to slowly build in him.

"So how are the mothers?" Jacey asked Ashley, referring to Ashley's mother, Miriam, and Miriam's best friend, Leona.

Ashley laughed. "They're happy as clams. They had the time of their lives planning my wedding, as you know, since you were my maid of honor, and now they're engrossed in planning Roger's wedding."

"Roger's getting married?" Ashley had been briefly engaged to Roger Freeman, Leona's son.

Ashley nodded her head. "I'm happy to say Roger has finally found a great girl he actually loves more than his work." She took a bite of her salad and eyed her friend with interest. "So tell me, are there any wedding bells in your immediate future? Just say the word. Mother and Leona have become experts at planning weddings, and they'd love nothing more than to take charge of yours."

Jacey shook her head ruefully. "No, no wedding bells."

Ashley made a moue of disappointment. "I was hoping you'd be in love. It's a wonderful feeling, and I want you to know it too. Aren't you even seeing anyone?"

"Nope. No one." Love had certainly transformed Ashley, Jacey thought, gazing at her friend. She glowed with serenity and happiness, and for the first time in her life she was anchored and centered. Jacey yearned for the kind of love Ashley had found with Max, a deep, abiding love that was returned without measure.

Fighting an aching heart, she plastered a smile on her face. "Okay, enough about my nonexistent love life. Tell me, when are Miriam and Leona going to be able to start planning a nursery for the Hayden household?"

Ashley grinned from ear to ear and her green eyes sparkled. "Well, as a matter of fact . . ."

Jacey made a point to skirt the study and the sitting room when she came home. She went straight up to her room, took off her clothes, and slid into a hot, steaming scented bath.

She knew she had to see Philip sooner or later; after all, they were the only two people in the house at the moment. Barton and two other long-time members of the household staff had their own house on the grounds of the estate, which they went to in the evening after dinner. It stood to reason that she and Philip would meet sooner or later, but she wanted to give the two of them more time to be apart.

She certainly needed the respite, and she wanted Philip to have the opportunity to think things through. He needed to realize that they couldn't continue being lovers, and that instead, they should try for a distant but pleasant relationship. And he couldn't come to that conclusion as long as the two of them were lying in the same bed.

At least she didn't think he could. Lord knew, her brain certainly ceased to function when his arms were around her.

The gradually cooling water and the three quick rings from her telephone that signaled a call had been routed to her room finally forced her out of the tub.

Clutching a towel around her, she hurried into the bedroom and picked up the phone. "Yes?"

"Jacey darling, it's Mother."

Her voice sounded nervous and unsure, Jacey thought. As if she weren't sure whether she should laugh or cry. "Is there anything wrong, Mother? I thought you and your group would be on the road by now. Where are you calling from?"

"Well, actually I'm calling from Barbados. It's a lovely place, just lovely. Have you ever been here? I'm sure you must have been, it's—"

Jacey sank onto the bed. "Did I miss something? Does Barbados have autumn leaf tours?"

Edith cleared her throat. "No, of course not, but Robert . . . well, he thought it would be a grand idea if we came down. Before I knew it, he chartered a plane and here we are. Of course I have nothing whatsoever in my suitcase that's appropriate to wear, but Robert says we can buy what we need."

Jacey was silent for a moment as she fought back the urge to laugh. She was *really* looking forward to meeting Robert Gage. He had to be quite a man. "*We*, Mother? Is your whole group down there with you?"

"Uh . . . no. Everyone else went on to New England as planned, but Robert, well, he . . ."

Jacey decided to end her mother's ordeal. "I

think going to Barbados is a wonderful idea, and I know you're going to have a great time. Just let yourself relax and go with the flow. Stay as long as you want, but when you get back, I want to meet Mr. Gage."

"Yes, he says he wants to meet you too, darling. Oh, dear, I almost forgot to ask. How did last night go?"

"Perfectly. Philip got exactly what he wanted."

"That's wonderful, darling. Be sure and tell Philip how happy I am for him."

"I will, and you tell Mr. Gage to take good care of you."

Edith cleared her throat. "Yes, well, I don't seem to have to tell him anything."

Jacey smiled, reflecting that Robert Gage sounded like the perfect man for her mother. "Good-bye, Mother."

"Good-bye, darling."

The smile lingered on her face as she toweled off, then dressed comfortably in a pair of gold wool slacks and a tunic-length cashmere sweater of the same color. She added small hoop earrings, then brushed her hair until it lay gleaming around her shoulders.

When a knock sounded on her door, her smile faded and her heart skipped a beat. Anticipation pulsed through her as she walked slowly to the door and opened it.

"Barton?" She hoped her disappointment didn't show. She had expected, *wanted*, Philip to be standing on the other side of the door.

Sure she could have a distant but pleasant relationship with him, she thought with wry despair. She needed to get out from under his roof as soon as possible and make sure she never spent another night here again.

Barton, his expression one of the utmost dignity, nodded to her. "I trust you found your shoes?"

"Shoes?" she asked blankly.

"This morning I discovered one of your gold satin pumps in the sitting room, and later, I found the other in Mr. Killane's room."

"Oh." Her shoes and their whereabouts had been the last thing on her mind.

"I took the liberty of bringing them to your room and placing them in your closet."

Even if she were so inclined, she didn't see much point in making up an elaborate excuse. And she wasn't so inclined. "Thank you, Barton. That was very kind of you."

He nodded again, his reserved, slightly haughty demeanor never once slipping. "Mr. Killane asked me to inquire if you would join him in the sitting room before dinner."

Her hand tightened on the doorknob. It appeared that her respite from Philip had ended. "Tell him that I'll be down shortly."

"Very good, Mrs. Killane."

She did a double take, then stared at him, flabbergasted. "How did you know?"

An ever so discreet sparkle appeared in his eyes. "To be a truly good butler, one must not only be intuitive, one must be observant. In that way, one can better serve one's employers."

For the life of her, she couldn't think of anything to say, and luckily he didn't seem to expect anything of her.

"If I may say so, Mrs. Killane, I was very glad to see you come home. A day hasn't gone by that I haven't worried over your separation from Mr. Killane. If there is anything I can do for you or—"

She gathered herself together and managed a smile. "It's very kind of you to care, Barton, but no, there's nothing. And by the way, you are most definitely an excellent butler. In case no one has told you lately, this family is extremely fortunate to have you."

He actually smiled, a full-face, transforming smile. "Thank you, Mrs. Killane. I've always felt that way too."

She was smiling when she shut the door, but it was with sadness that she reflected that Barton was the first person to ever call her Mrs. Killane, and more than likely he would be the last.

Standing by the fireplace, waiting for Jacey, Philip stared unseeingly into the flames. Anger gnawed at him, and, at the same time, an old, heavy weight of fear had settled in his gut.

She was going to leave—he could sense it—unless he did something to stop her. He had felt her withdrawing from him this morning after they had made love, and he was determined to stop her before she withdrew anymore.

But what could he do? She wouldn't believe him if he told her he loved her. Chances were, she wouldn't even care.

He kicked a log with the heel of his shoe, sending it rolling to the back of the fireplace. Fiery sparks flew upward. Dammit, he had to do something. He just wished he knew what.

Truth was the only answer, his only hope. If he was tactful and reasonable and laid out exactly how he felt about her, she might change her mind. He prayed she would, because it was all he could think to do.

• • •

If Barton was so intuitive, Jacey thought, making her way downstairs to the sitting room, then he would know that Philip didn't love her. But in his starched, reserved manner, he still seemed pleased that she and Philip had spent the night together. Great, she reflected sourly. In addition to everything else, she had the weight of Barton's expectations on her shoulders. The sooner everyone knew she was going to leave, the better.

As Barton had told her, Philip was indeed waiting for her. He was standing by the fire, dressed in jeans and a dark blue striped shirt, its neck open and the sleeves rolled up. Equal parts of masculinity and anger radiated in waves from him.

Unaffected, Douglas snored blissfully at his feet.

She wasn't as lucky. Every nerve she possessed was pulled to its tightest. She needed to say what she had to say and then get away from him as quickly as possible, she decided. First, though, she needed to try to break the tension that pulsed in the air around them. "Do you think Douglas gets enough rest?" she asked with an attempt at light banter.

"How was your lunch?"

Okay, she thought. No light banter. "It was great seeing Ashley again. I haven't seen her since her wedding, so we had a lot to catch up on."

"Did you tell her you'd been sick?"

"No."

"Why not?"

She rolled her shoulders uneasily. She hadn't expected this line of questioning. In fact, she hadn't expected him to question her at all about her lunch. "What would be the point of telling her now?"

"Because she cares about you, Jacey. Because it might be of more than passing interest to her that you almost died."

"Why worry her when the worst is past?"

He slapped his forehead with the palm of his hand, his gesture clearly sarcastic. "Oh, right. I forgot. You'd rather die alone than worry anyone."

She eyed him steadily. "We've been through all of this, Philip. What's gotten you upset again?"

He ran his hand around the back of his neck. Lord, he even had knots there. He dropped his hand. "I may not have mentioned it lately, but I've never stopped being upset about it." Jagged edges of emotion he couldn't control poked here and there through the evenness of his voice. Tactful and reasonable, he reminded himself. "How are you feeling? I mean, last night wasn't too much for you, was it?" He was genuinely concerned, though he had to admit that his concern had come after the fact.

"No, not at all. I enjoyed it." What a stupid answer, she thought, chagrined. She had sounded as though she were thanking him for an evening at the opera. She flicked her tongue across her dry bottom lip. "Listen, I might as well tell you that I'll be going back to my apartment in the city tomorrow."

Anger flared up in him with a suddenness and a strength that stripped away all civility and left only the most primitive of instincts. He wasn't going to lose her. He *couldn't*. "No. *No*, you won't."

"Excuse me?"

"You're not going to your apartment. What's more, you're not going to travel anymore, at least not alone. But above all, you're going to stay right here." He looked at her stunned face and almost cursed. So much for tact and reasonableness. But he had gone too far to turn back now. He pointed a stern finger at her. "And I'll tell you something else you're *not* going to do. You're *not* going to get a divorce."

If he had hit her, she couldn't have been more shocked or astounded. "Which outrageous statement would you like me to address first, Philip? I mean, would you like me to take them in order? On second thought, maybe reverse order might be better. What in the hell do you mean, I'm not going to get a divorce?"

He had blown it. He had really blown it. In his fear of losing her again, he had reverted to the scared, uncertain young man he had been ten years before when he had stormed into her room and told her exactly what she was going to do. He had long, dark, bleak years behind him to show him that it hadn't worked then, and there was no way it was going to work now. This time it wouldn't be ten years without her— it would be the rest of his life. The knowledge scared him to death, and fighting against the terror, his mind scrambled to find a way to save himself.

When he didn't answer her, she said, "Philip, help me out here. I'm lost. Do *you* want to be the one to get a divorce? Is that it? And what's this about my staying here and not traveling?"

He shook his head, experiencing an inexpressible helplessness. He said the first thing that came to his mind. "On second thought, maybe we should get a divorce. It would give us the opportunity to do it all over again, because that's what we need."

Her light laugh held raw nerves. "If you don't mind, there are certain things I'd rather not go through again."

His teeth clenched so hard, pain shot to his head. But he was already in so much pain, he barely noticed it. He had never felt more miserable or unsure in his life. He had managed to convince twenty hostile stockholders to see things his way, but he didn't have a chance with Jacey. "You want to leave because of what happened between us last night, don't you?"

The abruptly introduced subject made her take a deep breath. Telling him she was going to leave had been hard enough, but now he wanted to talk about something that struck at the core of her heart. He wanted to talk about last night, a relatively short space of time when she had freely given herself to him in every way. But he hadn't known the love that had backed her actions, and now she had to steel herself to put that time behind her.

"Why are we suddenly having trouble communicating?" she asked, half desperate, half incredulous. "We managed to work together all week, and now either you're not listening to me, or I'm not listening to you. So *listen*. I told you this morning that I wanted what happened. It was great, but we both know you can't build a relationship on sex, and since that's all there is between us . . ." She trailed off, perilously close to losing her composure and unable to continue with anything close to equanimity. She was giving him an out that was all but gift wrapped. He just had to reach out and take it.

His elbow propped on the mantel, his hand clenched and unclenched. "Sit down, Jacey."

It was another order, but she decided the idea had its merits. She felt as if her backbone were in imminent danger of dissolving. She dropped onto the couch and glanced vaguely around the room. Maybe a drink would be a good idea, she thought. She was well enough, and Lord knew she needed *something* to fortify her.

He came away from the mantel and stood before her, looking down at her, his fisted hands now hidden in his pockets. "We were both so damned young when you came to my room that summer night. . . . But, Jacey, I didn't feel guilty."

He was trying to make her feel better. Oddly, his kindness hurt. She looked away from him, afraid something in her expression would give her away. "You don't have to say that."

"Yes, Jacey, I do. The fact that I didn't say that and a lot more then or since is a sin I'll carry to my grave. Look at me."

She shook her head. She wasn't up to an in-depth review of their past mistakes and an analysis of why it wouldn't work between them now. "I'd rather not talk about this. It's history."

Frantic to find some way to reach her, he squatted down in front of her, and with his long fingers against the side of her cheek, he gently turned her face so that she looked at him. "It's history that's still affecting us. After being with you all that night, I was desperate to keep you. It was why I rushed the wedding, and why I fell apart when you wouldn't move out of the house and come live with me."

He fell apart? No, that couldn't be right. She was having trouble understanding him. She heard the words, but she was sure her interpretation of their meaning was wrong.

He eyed her with concern. She was looking at

him as if he were speaking a foreign language. "I'm not saying this well, am I? What's more, I'm doing the same thing I did ten years ago—the *exact* thing I didn't want to do. I'm trying to bulldoze you, and I'm making a mess of things."

She had no idea what he was trying to do, but she knew that her resolve to leave went only so far, and if he continued as he was, she was afraid she was going to disgrace herself and embarrass him. "Philip, forget any explanations or apologies. I don't need them. Just tell me what you'd like me to do about the divorce and I'll do it."

Every time she said the word *divorce*, he felt as though something died in him. But the strength of his love for her made it impossible for him to give up. "You're going to have to humor me, Jacey. There are things I need to say to you, things I need you to hear."

"But—"

"Please listen."

It was the *please* that got her. That and the imploring expression on his face and in his tone. Before this moment she wouldn't have been able to envision him pleading for anything. She loved him, and she couldn't deny him. Reluctantly she nodded.

"Ten years ago I wasn't only young, I was a thick-headed fool with too much ego and not enough sense, and because of it, you and I never had a chance. But we do now if I don't mess it up too badly, because just like then, I'm desperate to keep you. Don't get a divorce, Jacey."

She didn't move, didn't breathe. Disbelief warred with hope.

He read the disbelief in her expression. "It's true. If I lose you again, my victory with the stockholders last night will mean nothing." He shifted, coming forward on his knees so he was directly in front of her. Needing with everything that was in him to touch her, he took her hand. "Marry me again, Jacey, only this time in a church with flowers, beautiful music, and you in a long white dress. But in the meantime, please, *please* don't leave me."

Her heart pounded like a drum. She had understood the words this time, but doubt remained. The long, lonely years had taken their toll on her. He had said a lot, but he had left out one very important thing. "Why, Philip? Why the abrupt change? Because we happen to be good together in bed?"

He smiled shakily, crookedly. "We're flat-out damned incredible together in bed, but that's beside the point right now. Jacey, I didn't know what love was ten years ago, and the intervening years didn't teach me either. But you've been an obsession that's haunted me to the point that I've never been able to have any kind of a relationship with any other woman, so I dedicated myself to my work. And when you showed up again and I knew you'd be staying awhile . . ." He shook his head as words temporarily deserted him. He tried again. "Having you here again began to work on my mind. I wanted you so damned bad. And then when you told me you'd been sick and had nearly died, I almost went over the edge"—his voice broke, and his next words were spoken in a whisper—"because I realized I'd never be able to go on if I lost you."

Tears stung his eyes. The importance of that moment and of her was staggering. He was about to lay bare his heart, something he had never in his life done. But suddenly he wasn't afraid, because he knew he couldn't do anything less. His grip tightened on her hand. "I'm on my knees to you, Jacey. I'm sorry for the past, but there's nothing I can do about it. The future is different, though, I want the opportunity to share your future. I love you."

He'd said what she had needed to hear. "You love me?"

"Completely. Totally. Please, Jacey, marry me again and live with me for the rest of our lives."

Her laughter contained a sob of happiness. Finally it had all sunk in, and she felt light-headed with exhilaration. "You want to marry me again?"

The laughter caught Douglas's attention. His ears lifted, and he opened one eye. His beloved master was on his level, he noted with interest. He levered his bulk upright, ambled over, plopped his behind down beside Philip, and looked back and forth between the two of them expectantly.

Philip's whole attention was riveted on Jacey, and worry creased his forehead. "If you don't like the idea, we don't have to have another wedding. I know you don't love me yet, but—"

She reached out and tenderly framed his face with her hands. Her touch silenced him quicker than words could have.

"I've always loved you, Philip, right from the first moment I saw you when I was thirteen years old. And despite the impossible odds, despite the fact that I tried to will it otherwise, my love has grown stronger with the years. It drove me right back home to you."

"Thank God," Philip whispered reverently. *He wasn't going to lose her.*

She smiled. "I love the idea of another wedding. I hated our first wedding, that secret, rushed affair in the judge's chamber. And I was so scared."

The tears that had threatened flooded his eyes, but instead of blinking them away, he let them stay. Because of Jacey and the miraculous, all-consuming love he felt for her, he could admit to himself and to her that he did cry. "I was scared too. Scared out of my mind. I wish I'd told you."

She viewed with awe the sight of tears in his usually hard, always dark eyes. One after the other the tears began to slip down his face. She caught one of them on the tip of her finger. "I wish you had too," she said softly, "but we can't keep on blaming ourselves for it. Because even if you had told me, or even if I had dredged up the courage to tell you the things I should have, we have no guarantees that it would have worked out between us. We both had a lot to learn, but we've done it, and now we're older and wiser."

"Not to mention lucky," he said, emotion clogging his throat, his eyes and face glistening wetly. "We have a chance to do it over again."

She smiled tremulously. "I think I'll buy the silver dress after all, and wear it instead of a traditional white gown." Her smile broadened at his shocked expression. "Don't worry. I'll have the designer make a jacket and a slip for it."

"When we're alone, will you wear it for me without the jacket and the slip?"

"Most definitely."

"You're everything to me," he said softly, reaching for her. "You're my entire world."

With a laugh of pure joy she slid off the sofa and into his arms. Her weight carried them backward onto the floor, and their lips joined in a long, deep kiss.

Douglas gave a bark of delight at the new game and raced around them in a circle.

And Barton, who just happened to be passing by the door, heard the giggles mingled with the barking and permitted himself a small smile. "At last."

THE EDITOR'S CORNER

Next month's lineup sizzles with BAD BOYS, heroes who are too hot to handle but too sinful to resist. In six marvelous romances, you'll be held spellbound by these men's deliciously wicked ways and daring promises of passion. Whether they're high-powered attorneys, brash jet jockeys, or modern-day pirates, BAD BOYS are masters of seduction who never settle for anything less than what they want. And the heroines learn that surrender comes all too easily when the loving is all too good. . . .

Fighter pilot Devlin MacKenzie in **MIDNIGHT STORM** by Laura Taylor, LOVESWEPT #576, is the first of our BAD BOYS. He and David Winslow, the hero of DESERT ROSE, LOVESWEPT #555, flew together on a mission that ended in a horrible crash, and now Devlin has come to Jessica Cleary's inn to recuperate. She broke their engagement years before, afraid to love a man who lives dangerously, but the rugged warrior changes her mind in a scorchingly sensual courtship. Laura turns up the heat in this riveting romance.

SHAMELESS, LOVESWEPT #577, by Glenna McReynolds, is the way Colt Haines broke Sarah Brooks's heart by leaving town without a word after the night she'd joyfully given him her innocence. Ten years later a tragedy brings him back to Rock Creek, Wyoming. He vows not to stay, but with one look at the woman she's become, he's determined to make her understand why he'd gone—and to finally make her his. Ablaze with the intensity of Glenna's writing, **SHAMELESS** is a captivating love story.

Cutter Beaumont *is* an **ISLAND ROGUE**, LOVESWEPT #578, by Charlotte Hughes, and he's also the mayor, sheriff, and owner of the Last Chance Saloon. Ellie Parks isn't interested though. She's come to the South Carolina island looking for a peaceful place to silence the demons that haunt her dreams—and instead she finds a handsome rake who wants to keep her up nights. Charlotte masterfully resolves this trouble in paradise with a series of events that will make you laugh and cry.

Jake Madison is nothing but **BAD COMPANY** for Nila Shepherd in Theresa Gladden's new LOVESWEPT, #579. When his sensual gaze spots her across the casino, Jake knows he must possess the temptress in the come-and-get-me dress. Nila has always wanted to walk on the wild side, but the fierce desire Jake awakens in her has her running for cover. Still, there's no hiding from this man who makes it his mission to fulfill her fantasies. Theresa just keeps coming up with terrific romances, and aren't we lucky?

Our next LOVESWEPT, #580 by Olivia Rupprecht, has one of the best titles ever—**HURTS SO GOOD**. And legendary musician Neil Grey certainly knows about hurting; that's why he dropped out of the rat race and now plays only in his New Orleans bar. Journalist Andrea Post would try just about anything to uncover his mystery, to write the story no one ever had, but the moment he calls her *"chère,"* he steals her heart. Another memorable winner from Olivia!

Suzanne Forster's stunning contribution to the BAD BOYS month is **NIGHT OF THE PANTHER**, LOVESWEPT #581. Johnny Starhawk is a celebrated lawyer whose killer instincts and Irish-Apache heritage have made him a star, but he's never forgotten the woman who'd betrayed him. And now, when Honor Bartholomew is forced to seek his help, will he give in to his need for revenge . . . or his love for the only woman he's ever wanted? This romance of smoldering anger and dangerous desire is a tour de force from Suzanne.

On sale this month from FANFARE are four terrific novels.
DIVINE EVIL is the most chilling romantic suspense novel yet from best-selling author Nora Roberts. When successful sculptor Clare Kimball returns to her hometown, she discovers that there's a high price to pay for digging up the secrets of the past. But she finds an ally in the local sheriff, and together they confront an evil all the more terrifying because those who practice it believe it is divine.

HAVING IT ALL by critically acclaimed author Maeve Haran is a tender, funny, and revealing novel about a woman who does have it all—a glittering career, an exciting husband, and two adorable children. But she tires of pretending she's superwoman, and her search for a different kind of happiness and success shocks the family and friends she loves.

With **HIGHLAND FLAME**, Stephanie Bartlett brings back the beloved heroine of HIGHLAND REBEL. In this new novel, Catriona Galbraid and her husband, Ian, depart Scotland's Isle of Skye after they're victorious in their fight for justice for the crofters. But when a tragedy leaves Cat a widow, she's thrust into a new struggle—and into the arms of a new love.

Talented Virginia Lynn creates an entertaining variation on the taming-of-the-shrew theme with **LYON'S PRIZE**. In medieval England the Saxon beauty Brenna of Marwald is forced to marry Rye de Lyon, the Norman knight known as the Black Lion. She vows that he will never have her love, but he captures her heart with passion.

Sharon and Tom Curtis are among the most talented authors of romantic fiction, and you wouldn't want to miss this chance to pick up a copy of their novel **THE GOLDEN TOUCH**, which LaVyrle Spencer has praised as being "pure pleasure!" This beautifully written romance has two worlds colliding when an internationally famous pop idol moves into the life of a small-town teacher.

The Delaneys are coming! Once again Kay Hooper, Iris Johansen, and Fayrene Preston have collaborated to bring you a sparkling addition to this remarkable family's saga. Look for **THE DELANEY CHRISTMAS CAROL**— available soon from FANFARE.

Happy reading!

With best wishes,

Nita Taublib

Nita Taublib
Associate Publisher
LOVESWEPT and FANFARE

Don't miss these fabulous Bantam Fanfare titles
on sale in SEPTEMBER.

DIVINE EVIL
by Nora Roberts

HAVING IT ALL
by Maeve Haran

HIGHLAND FLAME
by Stephanie Bartlett

LYON'S PRIZE
by Virginia Lynn

THE GOLDEN TOUCH
by Sharon and Tom Curtis

DIVINE EVIL

by the *New York Times* bestselling author of
CARNAL INNOCENCE and GENUINE LIES,

NORA ROBERTS

Sculptor Clare Kimball has a dynamic, individualistic style
that set the New York art world on end. But as Clare travels
back to her tiny home town of Emmitsboro, Maryland, she
must confront the tragedy of her father's suicide and the
half-remembered nightmares that suggest Clare, as a small
child, was the witness to terrible acts that give the lie to
Emmitsboro's image of homespun "niceness." Will Clare's
presence trigger fear—and retaliation—in those who know
more than they're saying about the town's dark side? Clare's
only ally is Cameron Rafferty, the high school bad-boy
turned sheriff. The wary curiosity Clare feels toward Cam
turns quickly into something else—a white-hot desire and an
unwelcome love. In Cam's arms Clare tells herself she is safe.
But Clare will pay a price for digging up the secrets of the
past—and will confront an evil all the more terrifying because those who practice it believe it is divine.

HAVING IT ALL
by
Maeve Haran

With a glittering career that will soon make her the most powerful woman in British television, an exciting marriage, and two adorable children, Liz Ward has everything she's always wanted . . . and no time to enjoy it. Tired of missing out on bedtime stories, family dinner, and slow sex, Liz decides to stop glossing over the guilt and panic of trying to do it all. She's going to find a new way to get the happiness and success she wants, on her own terms. But it's a search that will send shock waves not only through her life but through the lives of the family and friends that she loves.

"Funny, poignant and true . . . reveals everything we won't admit about being a working woman." —Rosie Thomas, author of ALL MY SINS REMEMBERED.

A British bestseller in its first American edition.

HIGHLAND FLAME
by
Stephanie Bartlett
author of
HIGHLAND REBEL

In this stand-alone ''sequel'' to HIGHLAND REBEL, Catriona Galbraith and her beloved husband Ian depart Scotland's Isle of

*Skye after their fight to win justice for the crofters is victorious.
But when tragedy leaves Cat a widow, she is thrust into a new
struggle—a battle between Texas farmers and the railroads—and
swept by fate into passion more powerful than she'd ever known.
Can the dreams that died with Ian be reborn in a new land and in
the arms of a new love?*

Will hesitated at the foot of the steps to his office, breathing in the dusty sweetness of the autumn twilight. Catriona
hadn't wanted to leave Geordie, but the lad rode off alone
into the prairie. Will had insisted on driving Catriona into
Arlington to the mortician. Knowing how she'd acted when
Ian died, he was surprised when she agreed.

Will knew he ought to go on to the livery, get the buggy,
and drive Catriona home as he'd promised. But somehow he
just couldn't bear the thought of leaving her there and
driving back to town alone. As they stood together on the
plank sidewalk, the weight of her hand on his arm was his
only link to life, to sanity. She understood his sense of loss as
no one else ever could. He cleared his throat and turned to
her. "I—would you be insulted if I suggested stopping at the
office for a few minutes? I keep a bottle of whiskey there, and
I think we could both use a drink."

Her lovely face turned up toward his, drawn and pale from
their long ordeal, but marked by an odd calm. "Aye, I could
use a taste at that."

He guided her up the steep steps and unlocked the door,
fumbling inside for a lamp and a match. Air warmed by
the afternoon sun surrounded him with familiar scents of
leather and carbolic as the wick caught and a circle of light
flared around them. Carrying the lamp, he led the way into
his private office. He set the light on a corner of the desk and
pulled up an armchair for Catriona.

She dropped into it with a delicate sigh, leaning her head
against the high back and closing her eyes.

He seated himself in the desk chair, then delved in the
bottom desk drawer for the flask. The cork rolled to a stop on
the thick green blotter, and he poured an inch of the brownish liquor in the only glass and set it in front of Cat. He tipped

the bottle to his lips, savoring the trail of fire burning all the way to his belly.

But even that couldn't erase the image of Molly stretched across the bed she'd shared with Geordie, a child dying giving birth to another child. What kind of world was it where such things could happen?

He stood and paced to the window, seeing but not seeing the molten gold of the sunset spreading across the horizon, drawing starry darkness down after it. Sudden frustration surged through him at the senselessness and waste, at his own helplessness. All his skill hadn't saved her. There was just too much he didn't know. He pitched the flask with all his might against the wall. It crashed, showering fragments of glass and drops of whiskey onto the wooden floor. "Goddammit, I shouldn't have let them die!"

Catriona turned her tear-stained face, eyes wide and her mouth open. After a moment her lips set in a grim line and her eyes narrowed. "And who would you be to decide that? God himself? Face it, man, you couldna save them. No one could."

Her words arrowed into him, through all the scars, the years of armor, opening all the wounds anew. Tears burned a trail of acid down his face. And now he must add shame, the shame of showing his impotence before this woman, the woman he cared more about than anyone else in the world. He sank down into the chair and turned his face away, unwilling to look into her accusing eyes.

Then suddenly her arms were around him, pressing his face to the soft warmth of her bosom. Her kindness dissolved what was left of his calm. He pressed against her, letting the tears flow, losing himself in his grief. Nothing would bring back Molly or her son, or Ian, or a host of others he'd lost through the years. He'd become a doctor to save lives, without ever counting the cost of those he failed to save.

Catriona was right—he was only a man, not a god. He'd done his best, all he could do, and it was time to stop carrying around the ghosts of those who'd died in his care. At last, after he'd spent the grief of years, the tears stopped and he sat for a moment, enjoying a deep sense of peace.

Then a slow awareness returned. He held a woman in his arms, a woman he'd dreamed of holding, a woman he loved. Without loosening his arms he leaned back in her embrace and turned his face up toward hers.

Tears jeweled her dark lashes, and her soft lips trembled, but something more than pain or compassion hid in her dark blue eyes.

Desire flamed through him as he stood and cupped her face in both hands. Beyond thought, he bent and pressed his lips to hers, breathing in the mystery of her woman-musk.

With a soft groan she wound her arms around his neck, and he drew her to him, marveling at the softness of her breasts, her belly, her thighs pressing against him. With a sigh he released her, then scooped her in his arms and carried her to the cot in the corner.

The narrow bed protested at the weight pressing down on it. Catriona sank back into the softness, floating in an urgency of desire. She clung to his lips, drinking in his kisses, greedy for the whiskey taste of his mouth, his tongue. His mouth burned kisses down her throat.

Passion smoldered low in her belly, a delicious agony of fire longing to be quenched. One hand molded her skirt over her hips and down her thighs. His voice whispered out of the darkness. "Catriona, are you sure?"

A giddy joy, almost laughter, bubbled up in her. "Aye, never more than now."

Hunger possessed her as he ran the tips of his fingers over her back, her breasts, her belly.

She pressed her face against his shoulder. All the hidden longing of the last year welled up in her. As she melted against him, his lips sought hers in a gentle communion. He stretched his body beside hers. Pulling her against him, he curled around her, one spoon nestled against another, whispering her name. "Catriona, I love you."

LYON'S PRIZE

by Virginia Brown writing as Virginia Lynn
author of
SUMMER'S KNIGHT, CUTTER'S WOMAN, and RIVER'S DREAM

From the spellbinding Virginia Lynn comes LYON'S PRIZE, a tantalizing new historical romance with all the passion and color of its medieval setting. A defiant young Saxon beauty has sworn to kill the Norman knight who dares to marry her. But as we see in the following scene, she hasn't bargained for Rye de Lyon, known far and wide as The Black Lion for his legendary conquests at war—and with the ladies . . .

A burst of laughter erupted below, and Brenna's lip curled. Damn them. Damn them all.

When she reached the small square landing at the angle of the stairs, Brenna caught a glimpse of movement behind her. She turned quickly, her hand moving to the small poniard at her hip.

"Do not pull your weapon," the man said softly in the Norman tongue, which Brenna understood as well as she did her own.

Brenna sucked in a sharp breath. A Norman, and he looked much too dangerous. And close. Her fingers closed around the hilt of her dagger, and she pulled it from the jeweled sheath in a smooth, graceful motion.

"Stay where you are," she commanded sharply in French. "I have no intention of allowing you within a foot of me. Stay, I said, or I'll shout for my father's guard."

"From what I saw of your father's anger at you, he would

not lift a finger to stay me," the man replied with a sardonic twist of his mouth.

Brenna felt a spasm of fear shoot through her and was annoyed by it. Afraid? Of this man? Of *any* man? She jabbed the dagger in his direction.

"Stay away, or I'll slit you from gullet to gut!"

"Such sweet words, milady," the man mocked. He was only two stairs away now, and Brenna felt with her foot for the next stair up.

She looked at him closely. She did not recognize him and would have known if he'd been in Marwald before. No one could fail to remember this man.

He was tall, very tall, and his shoulders were broad, filling out the fine velvet of his tunic. A worked gold brooch held his mantle on one shoulder, and the hem swirled around lean, muscled legs. A broadsword hung from a wide leather belt at his side, seeming out of place with the elegant clothes, yet fitting for a man with such a hard face. Brenna felt a thrum of apprehension. A scar raked his face from eyebrow to cheekbone, slender and curved, giving his dark countenance an even more dangerous appearance. Beneath winged black brows, eyes of a startling blue pierced the air between them, thick-lashed and assessing.

There was an unholy beauty about him, a silent promise of ruthless determination and masculine appeal that made her throat tighten. She stared at him without blinking, fascinated in spite of herself.

"Do you approve, milady?" came the slightly mocking question, delivered in a husky voice.

Brenna straightened immediately. "Whoreson," she muttered in English before demanding in the French language he would understand, "Who are you? What do you want with me?"

By this time the man had reached the step where she stood, and she felt his proximity like a blow. Every nerve in her body screamed at her to flee, but she refused to act a coward. Particularly not before this mocking coxcomb with his fine clothes and neatly cropped hair.

"I want you, *demoiselle*."

Brenna stared at him. Her throat tightened as if a hand had closed around it. For a moment she thought she might actually faint. No. Not this man. He looked too hard, too savage. He did not look at all like a man who would be turned away with a few scornful words. It would take a great deal to turn this Norman knight from his purpose, she realized.

For the first time in years, Brenna was truly afraid of a man. She steeled herself. She could not let him know it. It would be fatal.

Her laugh rippled through the air, and she clutched her dagger tightly at the slight narrowing of his eyes. "Do you want me, sir? How very unfortunate for you." Edging up a step at a time, Brenna put some distance between them. She was not deceived by the man's seeming indolence. There was something about his pose that suggested a coiled spring. He was likely to leap on her without warning.

She reached the top step and flung back her head in defiance. "You won't have me, Sir Knight."

"I always get what I want."

It lay between them, that softly spoken statement, as certain and confident as sunrise. Brenna's mouth felt suddenly dry, and her heart slammed against her ribs. Yea, she'd been right. This man was dangerous.

"I'm afraid, sir, that you are doomed to disappointment this time." Her smile flashed briefly and falsely. "I do not wish to wed."

"That is of no importance to me." He moved at last, his powerful body shifting gracefully up the next stair. "Your king and your father have decreed that you will wed."

"And I do not obey lightly, sir." Brenna felt the last step at her heel, and took it. When she saw him move toward her again, she lashed out with the dagger, catching the velvet sleeve of his tunic and slashing it. Her heart was pounding with fear, and she hoped her legs did not give way beneath her. This man had not moved to avoid the blade, nor to catch her arm. He seemed completely indifferent to the threat she posed, and that was as infuriating as it was frightening.

"Get back!" she said sharply. She was no novice with a dagger; to amuse themselves, her brothers had taught her to fight. Now the lessons stood her in good stead, and she balanced on the balls of her feet as she faced this bold-eyed Norman. "Are you a fool to brave my blade?"

A smile curled his mouth, but didn't reach his eyes. "You toy with a dagger. When you think to become serious, I will take it from you."

None of her disquiet showed in her voice when she spat, "I am serious now."

"And would you stab me before the wedding?"

"Yea. I would slit you from navel to chin with no less haste," she hissed at him.

"Then do it, *demoiselle*." This time the smile reached his eyes, and he moved closer.

Brenna stared at him uncertainly. Perhaps he didn't believe that she really would use the dagger on him. He wouldn't be the first to feel the bite of her steel. There had been the overeager suitor who'd thought to dishonor her, thus forcing her into a marriage. He'd worn bandages on his arm for a month after. Now this bold man *dared* her to do it.

"I will," she said softly, and felt the hilt of her poniard slide reassuringly against her palm. "I've no love for Normans. Nay, I've no love for any man. 'Twould give me great pleasure to do what you seem to think I won't."

"Not won't." Amusement glittered in cold blue eyes, the exotic eyes of the devil. "Can't."

Stung, Brenna swung the dagger up, intending to slash his other sleeve and maybe draw a bit of blood along with it, just to show him.

To her astonishment the dagger was sent skittering down the steps in a clatter of metal and bone, and the Norman was gripping her wrist so tightly she gasped with the pain of it.

"Let go of me . . ."

"Aye, lady." He dragged her slowly to him. "When I'm through with you."

His face was only inches from hers, and she had no warning of what he intended until his dark head bent and he grazed her lips with his mouth. Stunned into immobile fury, Brenna couldn't think for a moment. He dared kiss her without asking permission! Few had done that and gone away unmarked, and neither would this Norman.

THE GOLDEN TOUCH
by Sharon and Tom Curtis
authors of
SUNSHINE AND SHADOW

"Ahhh, pure pleasure! . . . [THE GOLDEN TOUCH] is as tempting as one fresh, warm cookie from the oven—every page! Just couldn't get enough."

—LaVyrle Spencer

THE GOLDEN TOUCH is an amazingly beautiful story from America's most beloved romance writing team. This tale of impossible love between a small-town widow and a famous rock star reverberates with profound emotions and will tug at every one of your heart strings. In the following scene, Kathy Carter is quietly minding her musical instrument repair shop when her life suddenly changes . . .

She saw the motorcycle flash by her window and then heard it revving for a moment before it stopped down the street. *Someone thinks they're James Dean. What a royal pain in the neck.* Kathy rested her head in her hands.

She looked up when the door jingled. It was obviously the rider of the motorcycle—evident from the sand-colored suede bomber jacket and the helmet with a smoked glass visor he was pulling from his head. *Oh, no.* She knew it was just one of those silly small-town prejudices, but for her motorcyclists had a bad image based on old Marlon Brando movies where small towns like Apple Grove were destroyed by leather-jacketed hoodlums. He seemed to have a pack slung on his back.

But if the man in the leather jacket had mayhem on his mind, it was well hidden under the half-smile that was curving on his face. Specimens like that didn't make a habit of walking into "Kathy's Instrument Repair." Somewhere in the back of her mind, Kathy was surprised to feel a tiny synapse that meant that somehow she recognized him. Try as she would, she couldn't place the man. He was older than she—perhaps in his late twenties. Could he be one of her old friends from high school? Someone she'd been introduced to at summer camp? At college? Impossible. None of the possibilities rode motorcycles or wore leather. And the face before her was not one she would have forgotten readily.

He had nice features, though he wasn't what she'd call male-model, pose-for-perfume ads handsome. His face had too much character in it for that, and a glint of humor that hinted he didn't take himself too seriously. In a world filled with tension and pomposity, that quality was intently compelling. Dangerous. His hair was deep brown, full-bodied and shining. It was cleverly cut and longish, with an enchanting bedroom disarray from the helmet.

His cheekbones were high and wide-set, his jaw firm, and there was a tiny scar on his cleft chin. There was nothing particularly remarkable about his build—it was just the right amount slim and gracefully put together, though his shoulders had a look of strength to them. Good grief, why was she thinking about his body?

Feeling embarrassed, she raised her eyes quickly to his. They were pale blue—but, oh, what a pale blue, with an inner brightness, a calm study to them that was focused, just now, on her face. Instantly, she was taken aback. The man looked as though he could read every thought that passed through her head. Kathy didn't often find herself at a loss with someone, but to her dismay, she felt rather intimidated. She hoped none of that showed on the surface. Her hand strayed self-consciously to the straggling curls on her forehead. She lowered it quickly. Shape up, Kathy girl.

He had let her study him with a certain cool and rather amused patience. In fact, it seemed disconcertingly as though he were accustomed to that kind of survey. Then, as if he sensed that she had completed her catalogue of his features, he lifted the shoulder strap over his head. In the silhouetting light from the window, she saw that he held a battered guitar.

"I've got a problem," he said. "Maybe you'll be able to help me?"

The words might be ordinary, but the man in front of Kathy had an extraordinary voice. It was one beat quicker than a drawl, and marked by a delicately sexual rasp that licked its way into her body through the spine. She watched him lay his guitar on the counter, his voice echoing through her like the memory of a caress. Good Lord! What made her think that? All at once it occurred to her that she couldn't remember what he'd said to her. The effect of his voice had been so intense that the content of his words escaped her.

"Please?" she said automatically, meaning "I beg your pardon?" It was a central Illinois usage Kathy had picked up in childhood from her mother.

"Please?" he repeated quizzically. Then, correctly interpreting an idiom that was obviously unfamiliar to him, he said, "Oh, I see. Can you replace the tuning peg?" The voice again, a warm handstroke on her heart.

He lifted the neck of the guitar and showed her the broken peg.

The way a parent responds to a youngster with a scraped knee was exactly the way Kathy responded to a damaged musical instrument. She stood up, too quickly, and at the same time realized who she'd just said "please" to. She'd seen his face on Marijo Johnson's chest. She'd heard his luxuriant voice on her old gray radio.

"Neil Stratton," she said. Black spots shot into her eyes, spots that turned red, then green. Retreating blood prickled in her fingertips, and a hundredweight of dizziness spread its rapidly intensifying pressure under her skull. Heartsick and humiliated, she thought, Oh God, why didn't I eat? I'm going to faint! And she did.

Which was how Kathy Allison Carter, small-town instrument-repair technician and piano teacher, happened to wake up in the arms of Neil Stratton, songwriter, musician, and celebrity of international repute.

Regaining consciousness was an unpleasant business that was like swimming to the surface of a heavily chlorinated pool after taking a belly flop from the high board. She was short of breath, her legs felt numb, and her eyes itched. Opening them with a few blinks, Kathy found she was lying on the old burgundy floral couch in her back room with Neil Stratton supporting her in one arm and gently applying a warm terry washcloth to her temples with the other.

"Could you drink a little?" asked the wonderful voice.

She nodded weakly. The hand with the washcloth left her face and returned in a moment with a paper cup, which was pressed lightly to her lower lip. Sipping the water, she became slowly more aware of his hard-muscled arm where it made warm contact with her back through the thin cotton of her shirt. He was so close she could feel his clean breath on her eyelashes and smell the spring breeze and leather from his collar, his hair.

After she'd fainted, he had obviously picked her up and brought her to the couch—and then what? The washcloth, the water—he must have found the washroom behind the stairs, looked in the linen closet for the washcloth, found the paper-cup dispenser behind the door. A man of resource.

"You know, I could see it if I were Elvis," he said. Kathy could hear the smile in his voice. "I don't get many swoons these days. It was charming, though, if a little old-fashioned."

Carefully, she was lowered to the couch and a lemon yellow bolster pillow slid forward to support her head. A sudden and unexpected pang of disappointment shook her as his arms withdrew from her body. Somehow, paradoxically, the most important thing in her life became to disabuse him of any notion that she had fainted because he was—well, who he was.

Mustering one's dignity is something of a challenge when one is spread flat out and disheveled on a couch, but Kathy did her best. Forcing herself, she looked straight up into the blue eyes that were studying her with such fine-honed perception. "I know how it must have looked, but it wasn't anything to do with you. I was hungry."

OFFICIAL RULES TO WINNERS CLASSIC SWEEPSTAKES

No Purchase necessary. To enter the sweepstakes follow instructions found elsewhere in this offer. You can also enter the sweepstakes by hand printing your name, address, city, state and zip code on a 3" x 5" piece of paper and mailing it to: Winners Classic Sweepstakes, P.O. Box 785, Gibbstown, NJ 08027. Mail each entry separately. Sweepstakes begins 12/1/91. Entries must be received by 6/1/93. Some presentations of this sweepstakes may feature a deadline for the Early Bird prize. If the offer you receive does, then to be eligible for the Early Bird prize your entry must be received according to the Early Bird date specified. Not responsible for lost, late, damaged, misdirected, illegible or postage due mail. Mechanically reproduced entries are not eligible. All entries become property of the sponsor and will not be returned.

Prize Selection/Validations: Winners will be selected in random drawings on or about 7/30/93, by VENTURA ASSOCIATES, INC., an independent judging organization whose decisions are final. Odds of winning are determined by total number of entries received. Circulation of this sweepstakes is estimated not to exceed 200 million. Entrants need not be present to win. All prizes are guaranteed to be awarded and delivered to winners. Winners will be notified by mail and may be required to complete an affidavit of eligibility and release of liability which must be returned within 14 days of date of notification or alternate winners will be selected. Any guest of a trip winner will also be required to execute a release of liability. Any prize notification letter or any prize returned to a participating sponsor, Bantam Doubleday Dell Publishing Group, Inc., its participating divisions or subsidiaries, or VENTURA ASSOCIATES, INC. as undeliverable will be awarded to an alternate winner. Prizes are not transferable. No multiple prize winners except as may be necessary due to unavailability, in which case a prize of equal or greater value will be awarded. Prizes will be awarded approximately 90 days after the drawing. All taxes, automobile license and registration fees, if applicable, are the sole responsibility of the winners. Entry constitutes permission (except where prohibited) to use winners' names and likenesses for publicity purposes without further or other compensation.

Participation: This sweepstakes is open to residents of the United States and Canada, except for the province of Quebec. This sweepstakes is sponsored by Bantam Doubleday Dell Publishing Group, Inc. (BDD), 666 Fifth Avenue, New York, NY 10103. Versions of this sweepstakes with different graphics will be offered in conjunction with various solicitations or promotions by different subsidiaries and divisions of BDD. Employees and their families of BDD, its division, subsidiaries, advertising agencies, and VENTURA ASSOCIATES, INC., are not eligible.

Canadian residents, in order to win, must first correctly answer a time limited arithmetical skill testing question. Void in Quebec and wherever prohibited or restricted by law. Subject to all federal, state, local and provincial laws and regulations.

Prizes: The following values for prizes are determined by the manufacturers' suggested retail prices or by what these items are currently known to be selling for at the time this offer was published. Approximate retail values include handling and delivery of prizes. Estimated maximum retail value of prizes: 1 Grand Prize ($27,500 if merchandise or $25,000 Cash); 1 First Prize ($3,000); 5 Second Prizes ($400 each); 35 Third Prizes ($100 each); 1,000 Fourth Prizes ($9.00 each) ; 1 Early Bird Prize ($5,000); Total approximate maximum retail value is $50,000. Winners will have the option of selecting any prize offered at level won. Automobile winner must have a valid driver's license at the time the car is awarded. Trips are subject to space and departure availability. Certain black-out dates may apply. Travel must be completed within one year from the time the prize is awarded. Minors must be accompanied by an adult. Prizes won by minors will be awarded in the name of parent or legal guardian.

For a list of Major Prize Winners (available after 7/30/93): send a self-addressed, stamped envelope entirely separate from your entry to: Winners Classic Sweepstakes Winners, P.O. Box 825, Gibbstown, NJ 08027. Requests must be received by 6/1/93. DO NOT SEND ANY OTHER CORRESPONDENCE TO THIS P.O. BOX.